LEGENDS OF ELD
THE DRAGON OF ELFWOOD

A.D. Greer

Vanilla Raccoon Media
NEW YORK, NEW YORK

Copyright © 2017 by A.D. Greer.

All rights reserved. No part of this publication may be reproduced, distributed or transmitted in any form or by any means, including photocopying, recording, or other electronic or mechanical methods, without the prior written permission of the publisher, except in the case of brief quotations embodied in critical reviews and certain other noncommercial uses permitted by copyright law. For permission requests, write to the publisher, addressed "Attention: Permissions Coordinator," at the address below.

Vanilla Raccoon Media
www.legendsofeld.com

Publisher's Note: This is a work of fiction. Names, characters, places, and incidents are a product of the author's imagination. Locales and public names are sometimes used for atmospheric purposes. Any resemblance to actual people, living or dead, or to businesses, companies, events, institutions, or locales is completely coincidental.

Edited by Daryl Edelman
Cover Design by Thais Chu
Map & Other Artwork by Paul Kisling
Website & Other Artwork by Rob Yulfo
Book Layout ©2017 BookDesignTemplates.com

Ordering Information:
Quantity sales. Special discounts are available on quantity purchases by corporations, associations, and others. For details, contact the "Special Sales Department" at the address above.

Legends of Eld: The Dragon of Elfwood/ A.D. Greer – 2nd ed.
ISBN 978-0-9990143-0-1

This one is for my wife, Briana.

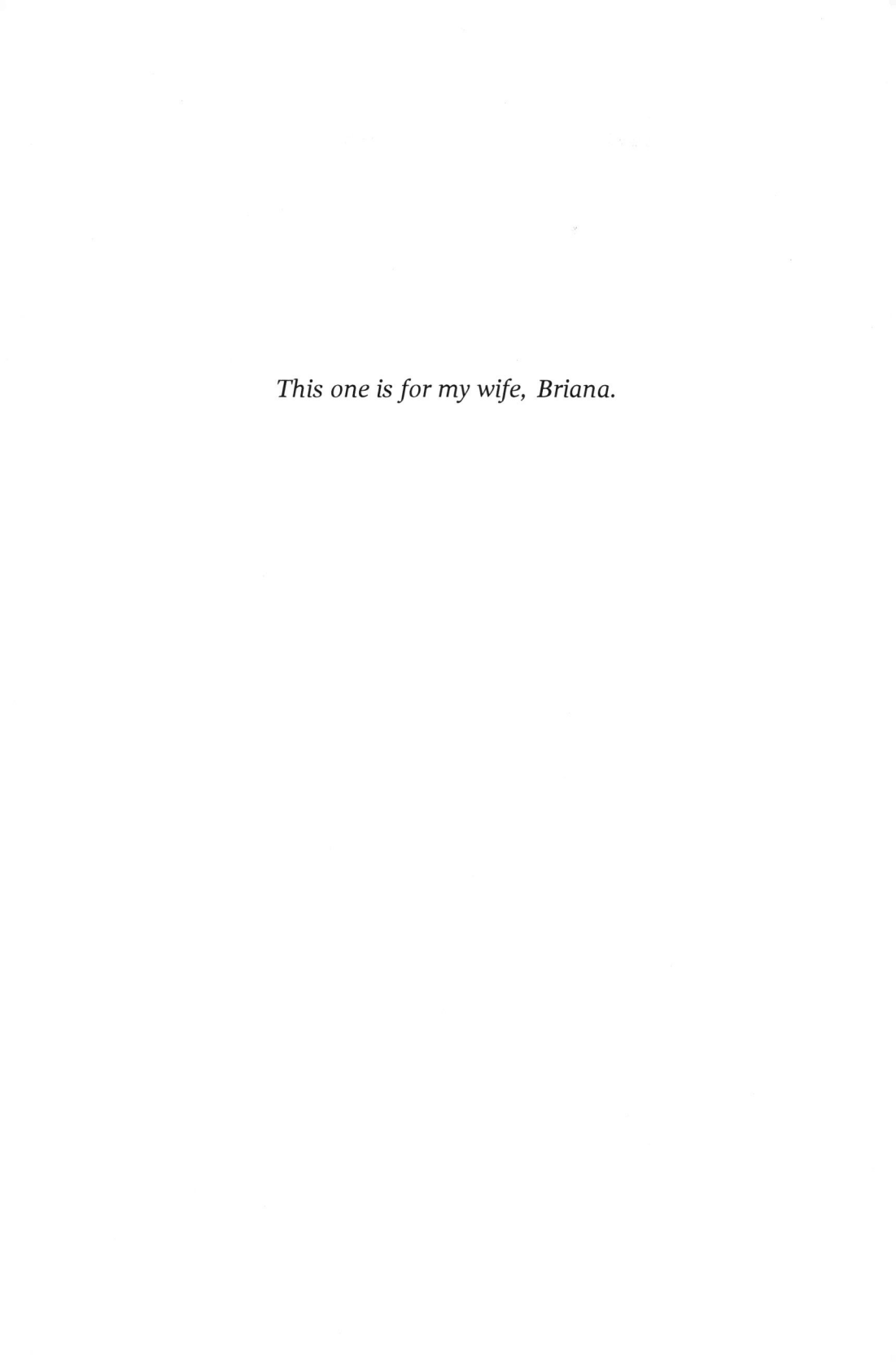

Contents

Chapter 1. Cole 1
Chapter 2. Eviction 5
Chapter 3. Glory 9
Chapter 4. A Bonafide Hero 11
Chapter 5. Sailing to Redlund 15
Chapter 6. Death's Edge 20
Chapter 7. Hikari Musha 24
Chapter 8. The Drunken Skeleton 30
Chapter 9. The Glue 39
Chapter 10. King Langsley 44
Chapter 11. Negotiations 52
Chapter 12. Double Dealing 60
Chapter 13. Way of the Warrior 67
Chapter 14. The Endless Forest 71
Chapter 15. Fortune's Fool 81
Chapter 16. Around the Campfire 85
Chapter 17. The Gate 91
Chapter 18. Elfwood 99
Chapter 19. Elven Hospitality 102
Chapter 20. The Prisoner 109
Chapter 21. Ambush 114
Chapter 22. The Tale of Il i'Tir 120
Chapter 23. Escape from Elfwick 129
Chapter 24. Parting Gifts 140

Chapter 25. Homecoming	148
Chapter 26. Second Chances	152
Chapter 27. Premonitions	158
Chapter 28. Rainbow Falls	165
Chapter 29. Through the Labyrinth	170
Chapter 30. Maisie	178
Chapter 31. The Bramble Tower	181
Chapter 32. New Lows	188
Chapter 33. Third Chances	194
Chapter 34. The Final Betrayal	200
Chapter 35. Rescuing the Princess	209
Chapter 36. Family Reunion	214
Chapter 37. Mad Dash	221
Chapter 38. The Dragon of Elfwood	227
Chapter 39. Fortune and Glory	232
Chapter 40. To Heaven's Peak	237
Acknowledgements	241
About the Author	243

Greymaw
Redlund Bay
Limen
REDLUND
Podunk
Castle Langsley
Langsley
Dust Valley
THE ENDLESS FOREST
Flounder
GREYSHORE
the Southern Throat
N
the Tranquil Sea
Bogs of Greyshore

CHAPTER ONE

Cole

Cole stomped down the muddy cobblestone streets of Flounder, muttering curses and thinking of great one-liners he should have said to those arrogant royal snobs. Who the heck did they think they were anyway? Cole was the most dedicated amateur adventurer they would ever meet in their lives, and they barely gave him a shot.

Stupid-pigheaded-dung-eating-orc-kissers will never regret anything more than turning me down for their quests, Cole thought. He smirked and made a mental note to use that diss the next time someone made fun of him.

Cole kicked a discarded fish skeleton into the gutter. It landed in a puddle and made a *ploop* sound that normally would have made him laugh. He was jovial more often than not, but today was different. Not even his most clever comebacks relieved his heartache. Cole felt hollow and lamented over his latest missed opportunity.

An hour earlier, Cole stood on a small wooden stage, in front of a crowd of nearly fifty other job-hungry mercenaries. Taxidermy monster heads mounted on the walls, decorated the adventurer's guild. There were dire wolves, giant bats, saber-tooth eagles, and a menagerie of other beasts Cole did not recognize. The fireplace was ablaze, but the expansive room was cold and uninviting.

Royals from neighboring kingdoms in need of heroic services sat behind an old wooden table, staring at Cole. He tried his best to remain calm. He wiped beads of sweat from his brow and combed it into his messy hair. The straw colored cowlick at the back of his scalp flattened momentarily then splayed up again. He lifted the hand-me-down ax he named The Ent-Eater from his shoulder, playing with the grip until she felt right in his hands. He'd been practicing all week for this moment, and it was time to show the world what he was made of.

Cole closed his eyes and took a deep breath.

A prince yawned.

Cole's eyes flashed open. He performed wild and vicious attacks against imaginary foes. He imagined himself standing on a mountain of slain ogres, chopping them down, a dozen at a time.

What the royals saw on stage was a large young man, wildly swinging his ax with about as much control as a riled up bull.

A slender marquis with a hooked nose and acne wrenched Cole from his daydream. Waving his hands, he said with a hideous smile, "Thank you. Thank you. That will be all."

"But I'm not done," Cole panted, confused.

A voluptuous viceroy whose chest seemed ready to pop out of her bodice squawked, "We've seen enough!"

"Oh, okay," he said, catching his breath. "Did I get the job?"

A few of the mercenaries giggled and snickered. An old count with a wispy halo of silver hair threw a warning glance over his shoulder. He turned to Cole and spoke with a voice hoarse from years of pipe smoking. "You have no lineage, no experience, and you're untrained," he said.

Cole nodded in agreement. "Yeah, but I got spirit. That's gotta count for something."

This time, all the mercenaries and most of the royals at the table laughed out loud.

Cole blushed with fury. "Don't laugh at me."

An earl with an extremely high voice wiped a non-existent tear from his eye and giggled, "I'm sorry, my boy. You're just so naive. I mean, look at you, thrashing about on stage like a fool."

Cole's mouth went dry. At a loss of words to defend himself, his mind spun in circles. He turned so no one would see how embarrassed and red his cheeks were.

A soft-spoken, middle-aged baroness wearing too much makeup cleared her throat. "Don't feel bad, my boy. There are many other professions to consider. Ones that could use a strong chap like you. Farming... fishing... do you fish?"

"How about being a stable boy?" the viceroy suggested.

The count nodded and agreed, "An honorable profession."

Suggestions about what Cole should be doing with his life twittered around the table.

"I don't want to be a farmer, a fisherman, or a stable boy. I want to be a hero," Cole said above the chatter.

"The world is full of heroes," the count said.

"The world can always use another hero," Cole replied.

Unabashed laughter erupted around the room. Cole couldn't hear it over the thumping heartbeat in his ears. The sound was like a war drum and when Cole heard the call, he lost all control and went into a rage. His muscles contracted, he bared his teeth, and the ax in his hands rose without him even realizing it.

"I said, don't laugh at me!"

Cole screamed, leaped off stage, and brought The Ent-Eater down on the table. He cleaved it in half with an ear-splitting *crack*! Quills and parchment sailed into the air. Roasted flounder, corn cobs, asparagus stalks, bread rolls, and butter spilled onto the floor. Plates shattered. Glasses broke. A single tin bowl spun on the floor, its ring humming over the shocked silence.

Cole wrenched The Ent-Eater from the timber and faced the room. Rivers of sweat ran down his beet-red face. Eyes burning, lungs deprived of air, he inhaled deeply and yelled, "My name is Cole! C! O! L! E! You better remember that name, because someday I'm gonna be the world's most famous hero. And when that day comes, you'll think to yourself, *darn it, I could have hired the world's most famous hero before he was famous, but I didn't because I'm stupid! STUPID!*"

His was the first and last tryout of the day.

CHAPTER TWO

Eviction

Cole lingered outside of a ramshackle stone building in the middle of Flounder's ghetto district. He didn't want to face his roommates, who probably expected he would have failed to book a quest. Again. He was sure they had snarky one-liners prepared to lob at him—as if he needed to feel worse about himself than he already did.

A pleasant aroma wafted out of the bakery across the street. His stomach gurgled. It was a blessing and a curse that his block always smelled of fresh bread, pies, and cakes. They were pleasant to smell, but a cruel tease for an unemployed adventurer. Hungry and broke, Cole owned nothing but the ax in his hands, the clothes on his back and the boots on his feet. He needed to find work soon or else he'd have to beg for food.

Cole exhaled a full-bodied sigh and made his way up to his apartment. He'd have to face his roommates sooner or later and he was done putting off unpleasant things. *How much worse could this day get?* he asked himself.

The apartment was the top floor of a three story building. He lovingly referred to it as the penthouse even though it was just a converted attic. Inside, there was a stool near the door, a wicker basket full of rubbish, and a chamber pot below a small window with a view of Flounder's idle docks. The place wasn't big enough for more than one person but it was occupied by three.

Cole's roommates, Dante and Jerome, lounged on their bed mats. Dante dozed on his, snoring like a pig. Jerome ran a skinny finger under his drippy nose and turned the page of the adventure book he read.

Cole stormed into the apartment and slammed the door behind him.

"Did you get the job?" Jerome asked without looking up from his book.

Cole picked up the stool and threw it out the window. The glass shattered. Someone outside screamed.

"I guess not," Jerome said and closed the book.

Dante rubbed his sleepy eyes and hoisted his heavy torso off his mat. Scowling, he exclaimed, "That was my stool."

"I'll buy you a new one," Cole said, pacing furiously around the room.

"With what money?!" Dante shouted. "You still owe us for the last three months' rent."

"I said I'll pay you back."

Jerome swept up the broken glass. "Maybe it's time you got a real job."

"Adventuring is a real job," Cole replied.

Jerome smiled at Cole with pity but said nothing. He picked up the last shard of glass with his bare hand and dropped it in the wastebasket.

Dante stood up and shook out his golden locks. "Don't you have to go on adventures to be an adventurer?" he asked.

Cole crossed his arms, stared out the broken window, and said, "It's just a matter of time before I get hired."

"Sure," Dante snorted.

Cole wheeled on him. "What makes you so great, Dante? You're just a cobbler."

Dante fired back, "At least a cobbler can pay his rent!"

Cole puffed up his chest, "When I'm a hero, I'll be able to buy this whole building."

Dante folded his arms. "And pay me back?"

Cole got up in Dante's face, which happened a lot, so Jerome rushed between them to mediate, which also happened a lot. "Cole, don't chop my head off or anything, but Dante's a cobbler. I'm a tailor. You? You're a what?"

Cole said nothing. He stared at his feet.

"Dante and I have been talking and we think it's time you moved out."

Cole looked up at Jerome. "What?!"

Jerome stammered, "We can barely afford to feed and house ourselves."

"We don't want to take care of you anymore!" Dante shouted.

Cole shook his head and said, "So that's how it is? After all these years? I remember when we first moved into the penthouse. You guys still believed in 'The Dream.' We wanted to be the most legendary heroes the world had ever known.

"Bards would sing of our heroic deeds for centuries. Maidens would fantasize about being rescued by us. Children would pretend to be us in the streets. Us! Cole and his band of monster slayers. Jerome versus the mountain troll. Dante and the yellow dragon!

"Now look at you. Dante, a cobbler. Jerome, a tailor. Where's your spirit?"

Jerome smiled pathetically. "We grew up. It's time you did, too."

Cole narrowed his eyes. "I guess I'll pack my things."

He picked up his ax. He was packed.

"Don't leave like this," Jerome said. "At least stay the night."

"No thanks," Cole said. "I know when I'm not wanted."

"You're right," Dante said. "You're not wanted."

Cole opened the door and looked back at his roommates with disgust.

"We're still your friends," Jerome said.

Cole thought of having the last word but decided it wasn't worth it. He slammed the door on his childhood friends and ran down the stairs. When he reached the sidewalk he wavered between running back up to them and begging their forgiveness or punching them in the face.

Dante and Jerome were the only kids he grew up with at the orphanage who didn't pick on him for being big. They were the only ones who entertained his dreams and wishes to rise above the poverty he was born into. When they gave up the dream, something in their friendship died. Cole lived in denial about their drifting respect for each other, but tonight the truth finally came to light. Just like the royals, Dante and Jerome thought Cole was a joke.

It was time to prove them all wrong.

Invigorated by anger, Cole stormed out of Flounder and hiked up to the crest of a hill. He stared down at the depressing city by the sea. It had been his home his entire life, but he found no comfort there anymore. Someday he may be homesick, but right now he was sick of home.

In a moment of clarity, Cole said to himself, "If no one will hire me, I'll just make my own adventure."

And with that, Cole bravely set off into the unknown, in search of glory.

CHAPTER THREE

Glory

Cole had no idea glory involved so much walking. He walked north along the coast of Greyshore. He passed through villages each more depressing than the last. By the end of the first day of his journey, he was exhausted, cold, and hungry. He foraged some wild berries and ate them, but soon after felt sick to his stomach and had a restless sleep. The next morning, he woke as tired as the previous night, but he kept walking.

By midday, he arrived at Podunk, a village thirty leagues north of Flounder. There wasn't any work for an amateur adventurer, let alone a professional. Cole walked to the next village, and the next, and the next. He walked through woods, past swamps, and over hills. Cole walked and walked and walked.

Walking gave Cole plenty of time to think. He fantasized about swords clanging off shields, bows loosing arrows, spears piercing armor, and maces bashing against his enemies. He imagined swarming masses of adoring fans celebrating his victories over vanquished monsters. There were moments of doubt when he wished for a warm floor to sleep on or a hot meal in his stomach, but the faces of Dante and Jerome and those arrogant royals reminded him his dreams were worth suffering for.

Cole came to an apple tree and his stomach rumbled. He plucked all the apples he could reach. He ate half a dozen and filled his pockets with the remaining apples. He ate the rest as he walked west through Greyshore. He stayed away from wild berries and kept close to freshwater, where he could drink and fish.

A week later, Cole found an abandoned canoe on a river bank. "Finally, some luck," he said to himself.

Cole pushed the tiny boat into the water and rowed downstream. He whistled a happy tune and thought, *Maybe I'll be a sailor. Yeah. I could travel the whole world!*

He didn't hear the man chasing him along the river bank, screaming over the rough waters, "Hey! That's my canoe!"

Cole navigated the boat down the river and docked that night in a small town named Port Limen. Dirt-poor, Cole was forced to scavenge for dinner. Not far from where he parked, Cole found a dead salmon. He assumed it was dropped from a local fishermen's daily catch. He chopped the salmon's head off with The Ent-Eater and peeled its scaly hide and ate it raw.

After the satisfying dinner, Cole sat on the docks, gazing up at the starry sky. Reeking of fish and desperation, and arms aching from rowing the canoe all day, he decided not to be a sailor. It was too much work for so little reward. Exhausted, he leaned back on his elbows and let his legs dangle over the side of the dock. Dreaming of adventure, Cole sighed.

Maybe the gods heard his wish because a gust of wind blew a paper notice into his face. It read:

WANTED: BONAFIDE HERO
FREELANCERS ONLY

CHAPTER FOUR

A Bonafide Hero

It was midnight, and all was silent but a breeze dragging dead leaves across the cobblestone sidewalk. Cole stood outside a decrepit building, wondering if he was at the right place. The dimness and cool air made him wary. He checked the address on the notice for the fifth time. Conceding he was at the right place—no matter how shady it looked—he pushed the creaky front door open.

Moonlight spilled into the dark room, illuminating dust and cobwebs.

"Hello?" Cole asked the darkness.

No reply came.

Cole did not notice Harold, the drunkard sleeping in the doorway, and stepped on him as he entered. Harold woke and screamed in agony under Cole's weight.

"Oh, my gods!" Cole shouted and leaped back onto the street. "I didn't see you down there. Can I help you up?"

Harold slapped Cole's extended hand away and shouted, "Don't touch me."

"I'm sorry, sir."

"What time is it?" Harold asked.

"The moon is at its peak," Cole said.

Harold yawned, stood, and stretched. He wore a faded scarlet overcoat, gray trousers that may have been white at one time, and high black boots caked with mud. Under his coat was a white vest polka-dotted with stains. He had long since lost his official ambassador's sash, but a shadow of it remained around the waist of his blouse. His unkempt beard was a tangled mess of ginger and white. His eyes wandered a bit as he spoke and his breath reeked of cider.

Harold stumbled over to the chamber pot in the corner of the room and relieved himself, intermittently hitting his target. He growled over his shoulder, "Are you a debt collector?"

"No, sir," Cole said.

Harold farted. "Then what do you want?"

Cole held out the notice. "I saw your flier. If you still need a hero, well, I'm available."

Harold shook, buttoned his breeches and turned. He looked Cole up and down, and scratched his bearded chin. "Where did you find that flier?"

"As luck would have it, it found me."

Harold walked over to Cole, took his hand, shook it hard, and said, "Harold of Redlund, the King's royal ambassador."

"Cole."

"Cole," Harold mused without releasing Cole's hand. "Just Cole is it? No titles?"

"Cole of Flounder."

"Never heard of it."

"It's south of..."

"I don't care where Flounder is. As long as you're a hero, I can leave this dreadful land. Greyshore is the most depressing country I've ever been stationed."

Cole nodded and let out an uncomfortable breath. Harold never stopped shaking his hand.

"You are a bonafide hero?" he asked suspiciously.

"Yes, yes sir," Cole lied.

Harold grunted, nodded as if he cared, and released Cole from his grasp to search the room for a new bottle of cider. Cole wiped his hand on his trousers. He wandered deeper into the room, past an overturned armchair. On the desk, cobwebs hung between towers of books and papers. If this was an adventurer's guild at one point, it had been a long time since it was used as one.

"You're the first in I don't know how many years to inquire about the King's daughter." Harold bent over, his rear high in the air, and dug through crates.

Cole upended the armchair, patted a cloud of dust off it, and decided to lean on it rather than sit.

Harold finally found a bottle of cider and grunted happily. "I had given up hope waiting for anyone interested in the quest. But the King sends my monthly salary, so I don't ask questions," Harold said. He bit the bottle's cork and pulled it out with his teeth.

"If I'm the only one applying, does that mean I get the job?" Cole asked hopefully.

Harold spat the cork onto the floor. "Sure," he said.

Cole went nuts and capered around the room, hooting and hollering with joy. It was as if with one simple word all the pain and heartache, years of desire and disappointment, all flew out the open door when Harold said, "Sure." *Sure*, the most beautiful word in the common tongue. *Sure*. It tasted sweeter than honey. *Sure. Sure. SURE!*

"Settle down, kid," Harold said. "You're making me dizzy."

"Thank you so much, Harold!" Cole exclaimed. "I won't let you down. When do I start? Tomorrow? Now? I can start now."

"Tomorrow's fine. I'll have to arrange for transportation and settle my debts." Harold paused. "Actually, I'll just arrange for transportation. Meet me at the docks. Sunrise."

"Sure!" It felt great to say. "Sure! I will! Thank you!" Cole hooted one more time and ran out the door, ecstatic.

"Whatever," Harold said, slurping down more cider.

CHAPTER FIVE

Sailing to Redlund

The next morning at sunrise, Nessa, a small brigantine ship, raised its sails and pulled out of Port Limen. The journey across the Tranquil Sea to Redlund would take a little over a month since they would have to travel south around the Bogs of Greyshore and through the Southern Throat to avoid the pirates of Redlund Bay. The captain of Nessa was a quiet but diligent man; he prepared for the worst and had enough supplies to travel there and back twice. He testified his crew was reliable, claiming each man came with at least a decade of experience. He promised Harold a safe journey at the stake of his honor and his own share of payment. Harold was less concerned about the odds of making it to Redlund and more concerned that the ship's hold would be stocked with enough cider. The captain assured him it would be. Harold paid him a small chest of silver circs weighing twenty pounds.

Once aboard the ship, Cole dashed about the vessel, weaving between the busy sailors. The crew was rough and weather-worn, strong from their years at sea. They spoke in a bewildering shorthand, barking orders back and forth between one another, and not politely either. Cole heard so many new words, he didn't know which terms referred to parts of the ship and which were insults. Each sailor was an irreplaceable cog in a well-oiled machine. They carried out their duty with a proficiency that reassured Cole this would be an easy voyage.

Cole leaned on the ship's railing and watched the town shrink in the distance. "Goodbye, Limen!" he shouted.

Harold approached, sucking on a new bottle of cider, "And good riddance," he said.

"I've never left Greyshore before." Cole had tears in his eyes. "For some strange reason, I feel like I'll never see it again."

Harold looked at the blubbering youth and snorted. He loathed sentimentality. It made him uncomfortable.

Harold elbowed Cole and handed him a small cowhide purse. "Here, kid. First installment."

Cole opened the purse and nearly wet himself. "There must be at least twenty circs in here!"

"Twenty-five now the rest later; the Langsley crown pays all its debt in silver. Redlund is famous for its silver mines, you know."

Cole didn't know.

"You can discuss further payment when you meet the king," Harold said between swigs.

Cole leaned his elbows on the railing. He propped his chin up with his fists, pushing his cheeks high enough to squish his eyes closed. "Wow," he said between sighs of joy. "I get paid and I haven't even done anything yet."

Later that night the crew played festive music. The orchestra of pipes, fiddles, a lute, and an accordion underscored the journey. Cole and Harold listened to the music as they ate and drank in their own corner of the deck. Both were a little tipsy and Cole felt possessed by the music. At the end of the song, he stood and applauded and whistled. Harold noted scowls from the crew. He pulled Cole back down to his seat. He passed the bottle to his young charge, who drank greedily from it. Another song began. This one, a little more mellow than the ones before.

"Tell me more about this quest," Cole said, his speech slurred.

"Well, the King's daughter is missing and he wants her back. You know the old story."

Cole nodded. He had heard that one before. "Wow. A real princess. I wonder if she's beautiful," he said.

"She used to be. Now, who knows? Forty years changes a woman. Not in a good way."

Cole thought neither men nor women aged well after forty years but didn't want to nitpick. He took a long swig from the bottle and burped.

"I can't believe I'm going to meet a king," Cole said.

Harold shrugged. "It's not a big deal."

"I wish I had something to wear. Like chainmail. Or... a cape. You know, something classy."

"Quit hogging the bottle."

Cole passed Harold the bottle, leaned back, and daydreamed under the moon.

Five weeks later at midday, Cole shook Harold—who was passed out in his cabin, clutching an empty bottle. "Harold. Wake up."

"Five more minutes," Harold answered groggily.

"We're here!" Cole exclaimed.

Redlund's capital, the city of Langsley, was named after its king. It bustled with activity as huge ships loaded and unloaded cargo. Seamen and merchants negotiated over prices.

Cole descended from the Nessa, more excited than a dog off its leash. Unhappy and nursing a headache, Harold lagged behind.

"Five weeks at sea," he lamented. "Miserable!"

"Five weeks? It felt like five years," Cole said, exuberant. "Look at this place! It's fantastic!"

Harold looked around. Saying it was *not* fantastic would be an understatement. The city was infested with crime, a reversal to what it was when Harold left for Redlund forty years ago. The Royal Guards who once patrolled the streets were nowhere to be found. Pirates, drunk and hungover from the previous night's debauchery, stumbled up to their ships. Thieves dressed in their gang's colors loitered, surveying the piers for easy targets to mug or pickpocket. Graffiti was tagged all over the buildings surrounding the docks. To Cole, it was a colorful display of art. To Harold, it was a warning.

"Keep an eye on your purse," Harold whispered to Cole. "Langsley isn't the safest city. Remember, you're not in Greyshore anymore."

"It seems safe enough."

"Looks aren't everything, kid," Harold said. "Trust your gut, not your eyes."

"Gut. Not eyes," Cole repeated. "Got it."

"I need to find a stable to arrange transport to the king. You have ridden a horse before?" Harold asked.

Cole had ridden a few ponies in his time but never had the kind of money to own a horse. Nonetheless, he nodded.

"Good. In the meantime, explore. We'll reconvene at The Drunken Skeleton. It's at the other end of Main Street. You can't miss it. I'll meet you outside at sundown."

"Main Street. Drunken Skeleton. Sundown." Cole repeated his instructions so he would remember them better. He turned to Harold and extended his hand. "Thanks again, Harold."

"Yeah, yeah," Harold said and left without shaking Cole's hand pushing through the crowded docks.

Cole turned to the impressive city. "Okay, Cole. This is your first time in a big city. Act casual." He took a deep breath and walked down Main Street, acting *casual*.

Unbeknownst to Cole, just a few yards away Harold was grabbed, gagged, and mugged by a gang of thieves. More ferocious than a swarm of wasps, they made quick work of him. They stabbed him repeatedly with their concealed daggers, robbed him of all valuables (his purse, royal ambassador's identification, and a bottle of cider), and dumped his body in the sea.

CHAPTER SIX

Death's Edge

Cole walked "casually" through the marketplace. It was sensory overload. Horse-drawn carriages hauling groceries roared down the street. There were beggars everywhere he looked. Many of them were children dressed in flea-ridden rags. They repeated the same sob story to anyone willing to listen. The few wealthy people Cole observed avoided the beggars and shopped with their servants. Children played whirl-a-hoop and miss-the-rope on the sidewalk. Tourists sketched their families standing in front of a statue of the King. Food stands advertised savory pies of roasted lamb and grilled vegetables. *Buy two pies, get one free.* Cole's heart was aflutter with excitement, but he remained "casual."

He passed a clothing shop with the two large display windows flanking its entrance. The windows showcased a mannequin in each window. One was dressed in male traditional garb, a white blouse and a scarlet overcoat, cream colored trousers, and high boots. The other was dressed in female traditional garb, a cherry dress with pink cuffs and slippers. The prices were staggeringly higher than anything Cole had ever seen in his life. A belt in Langsley cost as much as an entire outfit (boots included) cost in Flounder.

He walked deeper into the marketplace. He heard the clamoring of hammer against steel. Music to his ears, he followed the glorious tune coming from a small shack. He leaned on its half door and peered into the small shop. Cole peered through the haze and saw Bartimus, a dwarven smithy, peening a slab of steel. The short thick dwarf had a scraggly black beard, a bulbous nose, and wore shaded glasses over his large dark eyes. Being a dwarf, a subterranean race, Bartimus had extraordinarily pale skin. His shop sweltered with the forge at a temperature of two thousand degrees, but Bartimus wore long sleeves under filthy overalls to protect his arms from getting sunburned.

Bartimus thrust the steel into a tub of water. It hissed and Cole couldn't help but purr.

The dwarf noticed the large man-boy staring at him. "What are you gawking at?" Bartimus asked rolling his R's with a thick dwarven accent.

"I've never seen a dwarf before," Cole said. "You guys are small."

Bartimus stopped working, dropped his tools, and stomped up to Cole.

"Did you call me small?" the dwarf asked.

"Yep," Cole said with a wide grin.

Bartimus vaulted over the half door and punched Cole in the gut.

Cole said, "Wow! That's some jab you got there. I had no idea someone so small could hit so hard."

Bartimus punched him again.

Cole smiled and said, "Nice one, shorty."

Bartimus roared and threw a right hook but Cole caught it and said, "You pack quite the wallop, but you're slow."

Cole uppercut Bartimus and sent the dwarf into the air. His tailbone hit the ground first and then his head slammed against the pavement. Had he been any race other than a dwarf, his skull would have cracked, but his bones were as tough as rock. There would be a nasty bump on the back of his head for at least a week, but he suffered no concussion. When the world stopped spinning, Cole helped him to his feet.

"In all my years," Bartimus said in awe, "I have never been knocked off my feet."

Cole looked into Bartimus's eyes. He wondered, *will this escalate into a real fight or did I earn his respect?* After a moment of tense staring at each other, Bartimus laughed.

Cole sighed with relief. *Respect. Yay!*

The dwarf clapped Cole on the back with a large strong hand. The other he held out. "My name's Bartimus Thunderbeard."

Cole shook the dwarf's hand. "I'm Cole. From Flounder."

"Never heard of it."

"It's a town in Greyshore. Very small country."

"Humph. Is that how you arm yourself in Flounder," Bartimus pointed to The Ent-Eater, "with back scratchers? Ha. You need a real weapon. Come inside."

Despite its excessively hot temperature, Cole was happy to be in the small shop full of his favorite kind of toys—weapons. Impressive daggers, hammers, swords, shields, pikes, and armor—all crafted with dwarven precision—hung on the walls of Bartimus' shop. Cole was giddy. He secretly named each weapon.

Bartimus picked up a heavy double handed great-ax with a razor sharp steel blade. Cole snatched it out of the dwarf's hands and performed a few wild swings, forcing the dwarf to duck to save his head.

"That's good dwarven steel," Bartimus boasted. "Not your regular manmade garbage."

Cole admired the two-handed ax with reverence. It felt so right in his hands. Cole stared at his reflection in a nearby shield. He raised Death's Edge, the name he had given it when he first saw it. Seeing himself hold the most incredible work of art ever made, he knew he had to have it.

Cole dipped into his purse, "I only have twenty-five circs..."

"What's a warrior without a good weapon in his hand?" Bartimus asked.

"You're a wise little dwarf. How much? And no funny business, I'm not from around here."

Bartimus stood in front of the sign listing the prices of his merchandise to block Cole's view. According to the sign, great-axes went for ten circs.

"Tell you what," Bartimus said, "Since you're not from around here, throw in your old ax and I'll sell you mine for a special price. Twenty elders."

Five minutes later, Cole left Bartimus's shop admiring his new great-ax, Death's Edge. Bartimus stepped into the open doorway but stayed under the awning to avoid the sun. He waved goodbye. "Remember, if you want to get to the Drunken Skeleton, take a right at the corner, pass the fountain, and you'll be back on Main Street. Then head west. You can't miss it."

"Thanks, Bartimus!"

Cole disappeared around the corner and Bartimus's smile faded. "Sucker. Call me small," he muttered and slammed the half door shut.

CHAPTER SEVEN

Hikari Musha

Cole charged into Langsley's busy central square striking down imaginary foes with his new ax. Crossing the street, he nearly sliced into a horse-drawn carriage. The horses whinnied and the driver cried, "Watch it!"

"Sorry," Cole said.

"Moron!" the driver yelled, snapped his reins, and the carriage rolled off.

Embarrassed, Cole strapped Death's Edge to his back and made his way to a fountain in the center of the square. A statue of a stone cherub peed fresh water into the fountain's large basin. Graffiti by the local gangs scrawled on the fountain included a crude painting of a well-endowed woman with a finger pressed to her ample lips. Cole stared at the painting while pretending to tie his bootlace.

Unemployed and homeless people loitered around the fountain. Young couples, children, and other passersby tossed circs, copper or silver coins, into the basin and made wishes.

Cole retrieved a circ from his purse. "I wish to become the world's greatest hero," he said and tossed the coin in the fountain.

"Now it will never come true."

Cole turned and saw a short, chubby boy with freckles sitting by the fountain. "You said your wish out loud," the boy said.

"So?"

The kid rolled his eyes and said, "You have to think it. If you say your wish out loud, it won't come true. Don't you know anything?"

"I know how to teach snot-nosed-little-brats a lesson in manners."

The chubby boy ran away calling for his mommy, and Cole fixed his collar. He felt ready for any obstacle ahead.

A sharp piercing scream rang through the square. Cole wheeled around and looked across the street. A small crowd gathered beneath an oak tree in a church courtyard. Someone hidden in the tree wept. Cole dashed over.

"What's wrong?" he asked.

A peasant in the crowd said, "A little girl's stuck in the tree."

"I can't get down," the little girl shouted, hidden atop the oak.

Cole struck a pose and shouted, "I'll save you!" He leaped onto the tree trunk, wrapped his thick legs around it, and climbed up its trunk.

"Stop shaking the tree!" the little girl exclaimed.

"Sorry," Cole said, paused to let the tree center itself, and climbed as carefully as he could. The tree shivered again, and loose acorns and sharp twigs fell and hit Cole in the face.

"Careful!" the little girl yelled.

"I'm trying!"

"Hurry!"

Cole struggled up the tree. "How the heck did you get up so high in the first place?"

"I don't know," the little girl said.

Cole stepped on a weak branch and fell.

"What happened?" the little girl asked.

"I fell." Cole moaned.

The chubby boy pushed his way through the crowd of on-lookers and said, "Told you!"

A hush came over the crowd as a paladin stepped out of the church. Clad in golden chainmail armor emblazoned with the icon of his god, a sun encompassed by thirteen flames, the holy knight exuded superiority. Of medium stature but imposing presence, the olive-skinned man had silky black hair drawn back in a ponytail. He had a thin mustache drawn over arched lips that he often stroked with one hand. With the other hand, he gripped the hilt of his sheathed katana.

"What's wrong?" he asked in a foreign accent.

A peasant said, "A little girl's stuck in the tree."

"Don't worry," Cole said as he stood up and swept the dust from his clothes. "I got it covered."

"No," the little girl above shouted. "I want the hero to save me."

"I am a hero," Cole said.

"More like a zero," the chubby boy said.

"Where is this boy's mother?!" Cole shouted.

"Help!" the little girl shrieked.

The paladin stepped forward, but Cole stopped him. "I said I got this."

The paladin bowed in respect and stepped aside. Cole climbed the tree again. Halfway up, Cole reached for a branch and accidentally grabbed a squirrel's tail. Yelping some of the harshest curse words in Squirreleze, the frenzied squirrel bit his hand. Cole yelped, lost his grip, and fell again. Dust enveloped the crowd. The little girl above sighed.

On his back, his spine ringing with pain, Cole opened his eyes. He looked up at the mighty paladin warrior silhouetted by the sun.

"May I?" the shadow asked.

Cole sat up. "Ugh. Fine. Go ahead and try. No one could ever..."

The paladin swung his renowned katana, the Sun Sword, and cut through the tree's trunk. The tree groaned, tipped, and fell gracefully into the paladin's hand. Unassuming and much stronger than he looked, he lowered the tree gently to the ground. The little girl, a redhead with pigtails and missing teeth, hopped out of the tree.

The crowd erupted with applause. Cole fumed.

"Thanks, mister. You're the greatest hero ever," the little girl said and kissed the paladin on the cheek.

The crowd sighed, "Awwwww."

Jealous of the paladin getting praise meant for him, Cole addressed the crowd, "Well, it's not like he's perfect. He cut down that tree."

The paladin pushed the tree upright, closed his eyes, and whispered a gentle prayer. The oak glowed where it had been neatly cut, blinding all present. When the light dimmed, Cole lowered his hands from his eyes and saw the tree restored to its former glory. In fact, the tree looked healthier than ever. It was a miracle.

The crowd went nuts. The paladin knelt down at the little girl's eye level. He raised his index finger, and said in a stern but playful tone, "No more climbing trees you can't climb down. Promise?"

"Cross my heart," the little girl said.

The paladin smiled. "Good. Now run along and play," he said and sent her off with a pat on the tush.

She joined other kids in the churchyard playing tag as if nothing happened.

The crowd dispersed. Cole slumped his shoulders like a child, punished.

"You're a brave soul," the paladin said.

"Thanks," Cole muttered over his shoulder as he left the churchyard.

"May I walk with you?" the holy knight asked.

"I can take care of myself," Cole said.

The paladin let out an endearing full body chuckle. "Not as an escort," he said. "As a friend."

Cole and the paladin walked down Main Street in the direction of the Drunken Skeleton. As much as Cole didn't want to admit it, he was glad to be the center of attention. Or at least walking next to the center of attention. People stepped out of their way with awed admiration as the paladin passed. Cole thought, *So this is what it's like to be a real hero and get respect.*

The paladin broke the silence. "What brings you to Langsley?"

"I'm on a quest," Cole said.

"A quest?"

"Is that so hard to believe?"

"Not at all," the paladin said. "You are a hero, are you not?"

"You're darn right I'm a hero."

"Good. The world can always use another hero."

The comment caught Cole off-guard. It was the motto he lived by.

"I'm here to save the princess," Cole said.

"Princess?" the paladin asked, concerned.

Cole smiled. "That's right. The king's daughter is missing and they hired me to save her."

The paladin pondered for a moment, stroking his mustache. "I will aid you on this quest."

Cole stopped. "Oh, no. I don't need your help. And I'm not splitting the reward."

"If the reward is what you're worried about, you can keep the reward. I care not for fame or fortune, only a selfless duty to help my fellow man."

"Who are you?!" Cole asked, exasperated by the paladin's impeccability.

"I am Hikari Musha. Soldier of Light. Squire of our planet's star. A humble paladin of the sun god, Rey."

Cole faked a yawn and said, "Yeah well, that's very interesting, but I have to go."

"Where? I'll join you."

"Actually, I'm meeting someone. It's kind of invite only."

Hikari's smile faded. "Ah. I see," he said. "Perhaps our paths will cross again."

"Maybe," Cole said.

"What is your name?" Hikari asked.

"Cole."

"It was a pleasure meeting you, Cole," Hikari said and bowed. "I shall investigate the missing princess. Farewell." And with that, he turned and left.

Cole called after him, "No. Wait! I don't want your help!"

But Hikari Musha had disappeared down the street.

CHAPTER EIGHT

The Drunken Skeleton

As soon as the sun set, rain clouds appeared over the city. Cole stared at the skeleton perched on the tavern's sign above the front door. He wondered if it was real—and if it was, who it was? The thin bony fingers clutched a tankard filling with rainwater. The faded red letters spelling *The Drunken Skeleton* on the sign darkened as the wood soaked up rain.

Cole waited for Harold for hours. He paced back and forth, back and forth, back and forth, until reality sank in. Harold wasn't coming.

Thunder rumbled in the distance and Cole gave up waiting. He pushed the door open and stepped inside the most popular pub in the city. The packed raucous tavern was a vast stone complex. There was a large open hall on the ground floor, rooms to rent on the top floor, and a secret underground bunker for the most notorious gang in Redlund.

Thirsty, tired, frustrated, and cold, a tall tankard was definitely in order. Cole pushed his way through the mob on his way to the bar. He squeezed past tables of poker games. Cole peeked at a player's hand: four kings and a jack. It looked like a winner to him, but another gambler laid out a royal flush, and another, four aces and a king.

On any other night, Cole would have called out the cheaters, but tonight he didn't feel like much of a hero. He'd already spent the majority of his earnings on Death's Edge and had not thought of a plan to support himself in a foreign nation. He just wanted to forget how close he came to becoming a real hero. But as the chubby boy said earlier, he was a zero.

Cole waited ten minutes for a stool to become available at the bar and planted himself there. Leaky kegs were stacked behind the bar, and the bar top was sticky from spilled drinks. Cole reached into his purse, pulled out a circ, and ordered his first grog.

Twelve empty tankards later, Cole called out for another. The bartender was a rough man with tattoos creeping up his neck. He eyed Cole holding his tankard upside down over his open mouth, trying to shake out one last drop.

"You've had enough," the barkeep said.

Cole slammed his tankard down on the bar. "I'll tell you when I've had enough!" he slurred. "Do you know who I am?"

"No," the bartender said.

"I'm Cole. C-O-L-E. Cole."

To avoid an annoying conversation, the bartender refilled Cole's tankard. "Two copper circs," he said.

Cole spilled the few remaining coins from his purse onto the bar and calculated. The bartender slid the tankard across the bar and picked two circs from the pool.

"Don't forget your tip." Cole pushed another circ at the expressionless bartender who put it in his pocket. Cole put the rest of the coins in his purse, tied it back on his belt, and patted it. He lifted the full tankard in front of him and took a swig of the frothy grog.

The bartender turned to leave, but Cole grabbed his elbow. He regaled him with stories of his early triumphs. Five minutes later, Cole was still yammering. "This one time, when I was thirteen. No. Twelve..." As Cole tried to remember how old he was, the bartender prayed for one of the gods to put him out of his misery. "Maybe I was fifteen. I don't remember. But the point is, I defended the orphanage from a rabid wolf."

"Great," the bartender said.

"No one else stepped up. They were all afraid. Not me. I'm not afraid of anything. That's when I knew. I knew I was destined to be a hero," Cole went on and took another swig.

"Can I go back to work now?" the bartender asked.

Cole ignored the question. "The wolf was this big!" he exclaimed and stretched his arms their length to illustrate a wolf the size of a bear. Half of his drink flew from his tankard and splashed onto one of the gamblers at a nearby table.

Sarik, a guy who looked like trouble (and was), got soaked. His black cowl drenched from the top of his hood to the bottom of his cape. Sarik lowered his wet hood, wiping from the top of his shaved head and down his dark stubbly face. He looked at his wet palm as if it were drenched in troll bile. Sarik's eyes turned to slits. He took heavy, loud, deep breaths through his nostrils, a calming technique he learned from his childhood martial arts teacher (before Sarik killed him). He stood and turned. On cue, his cronies, each larger than the last, followed their leader.

Cole was still talking the bartender's ear off, but when the bartender saw Sarik and his cronies coming his way, he hurried off to the other end of the bar to clean up an imaginary spill.

"Where are you going?" Cole asked. "I'm not done telling you about the bully who used to pick on me at the orphanage."

Sarik tapped Cole on the shoulder and Cole turned to him.

"What happened to you?" Cole asked.

"Some idiot spilled on me," Sarik said.

Shocked, Cole said, "What a jerk. Did he apologize?"

"Not yet."

"You should teach him a lesson."

"Should I?"

"If I were you, I'd kick his butt."

"Good idea," Sarik said and slapped Cole's cheek.

The tavern hushed.

"Ow!" Cole exclaimed after the fact.

"Step outside," Sarik said.

The thud of a dagger striking a dart board broke the silence. A ruggedly handsome rogue pulled the dagger from the bull's eye. He was of swarthy complexion and wore an outfit as dark as a shadow. He turned his attention to the situation at the bar.

"Alright," Cole said, drained his mug, and belched. "Let's go."

Before he stood, the rogue caught Cole by the shoulder and pushed him back onto his stool.

"I wouldn't do that if I were you," he said, his voice as smooth as silk.

"Stay out of this," Sarik said.

Cole turned to the mysterious man. "Listen pal," he said, "Nobody slaps me and gets away with it."

The stranger nodded in agreement and threw an arm over Cole's shoulder to distract him while he stole his purse. "Let bygones be bygones. I'll pay for the damages," he said and tossed Cole's purse to Sarik, who caught it and smirked.

Sarik glared once more at Cole, snapped his fingers and returned with his cronies back to their table. The rogue ushered Cole to the other side of the bar.

"Thanks, pal," Cole said. "I think I'm too drunk to fight."

Sarik and his cronies eyed the pair from their poker table and the stranger said, "Let's get out of here."

The rain had stopped. The rogue escorted Cole, drunk and singing, out of the tavern onto the puddle-filled street. The city slept while he endured Cole's out of tune musical improvisation.

"Where are you staying?" the man asked and glanced over his shoulder to make sure they weren't being followed.

"I don't know," Cole said, splashing through a puddle. "I got stood up. You ever been stood up?"

"No."

"It sucks," Cole said and kicked a puddle.

"I know a cheap inn on the other side of town."

Inebriated and affectionate, Cole smiled moronically and said, "Thanks, pal. What's your name?"

"I have many names."

"Ooooh. How mysterious. What should I call you, Mister Many Names?"

"Call me Pal."

"Okay. Thanks, Pal," Cole said and stopped. "Hold on."

Before Pal could ask what was wrong, Cole barfed all over the cobblestone street. He wiped his mouth on his sleeve and said, "Now we can go."

Cole stumbled ahead of Pal, who caught Cole and steadied him.

"Why am I doing this?" Pal asked himself aloud.

"Because you're the best," Cole said, wrapped an arm around Pal's shoulder, and looked him straight in the eyes. "Let's be friends."

Pal wasn't good with affection and said, "Okay."

"You're my best friend."

"Cole..."

Cole sniffled and added, "You're my only friend."

"Don't cry. It's not a good look for you."

Cole wiped away the tears and snot dripping down his face. "I think I'm gonna be sick again."

"Oh, gods," Pal said.

Vomiting all he consumed earlier was painful and exhausting. Cole would not have been surprised if his boots came out of his mouth. He regretted every drink he had that night and every drink he ever had in his life. Cole finished and his throat felt sore and dry, but his skin was sweaty and cold. He stood up straight and wiped his mouth with his forearm.

"Pal?" Cole asked, scanning the empty street. "Where'd you go?"

Cole heard dull thuds and swift grunts, and the unmistakable sound of someone getting punched. It came from an alley across the street. He could barely make out four shadowy figures beating the heck out of some poor guy. When Cole's eyes adjusted, he saw Sarik draw a black dagger from his belt. He held it in front of Pal, who was restrained by the three cronies. Sarik pressed the tip of the black dagger against Pal's cheekbone, slowly inching up to his eye.

"Hey, you!" Cole shouted, stumbling into the alley.

Markos, the tallest, strongest, and definitely not the brightest crony said, "Hey, it's that jackass from the bar."

"Don't get involved, Cole," Pal said.

"Listen to your friend," Sarik said.

"He's my best friend and I'm not leaving him with you scum."

Falor, a weaselly little man with a grating high-pitched voice asked, "Did he call us scum?"

"I think he did. I think he did," said Pete-Pete. The third crony wore only a vest, so he could flaunt his muscular tattooed arms.

Falor asked, "We don't like name callers, do we?"

"We most certainly do not," Markos said.

"Oh, no we don't. Oh, no we don't," Pete-Pete added.

"Blah, blah, blah. Shut up!" Cole said leaning against the wall for support.

"Just go," Pal begged Cole. "I'll be fine."

"No. I've got this," Cole said, pushed off the wall, retrieved Death's Edge from his shoulder and paused. His face twisted and he vomited one last time before taking a moment to collect himself. "Okay, I'm ready."

Sarik flipped his black dagger into the air, caught it by the tip of the blade, and flung it across the alley. The blade pierced Cole's gut. He was completely indifferent to the pain, thanks to the grog coursing through his body. Cole pulled out the dagger and smiled at Sarik. "My turn." Cole unleashed a nonsensical battle cry and charged with Death's Edge raised above his head.

The cronies positioned themselves in a V. Pete-Pete took the front and Markos and Falor stood behind him. They drew their short swords and readied for battle. Sarik slipped into the shadows.

Pete-Pete ran forward and slashed at Cole's head. Cole blocked the high attack and pushed him backward and into Falor.

Markos flaunted his sword skills, flourishing it as he circled Cole. Pal tumbled behind him, and swept Markos off his feet with a kick.

Cole smiled. His new best friend was the real deal. The rogue dealt with Markos in seconds. He sprayed his fists around his torso until the man cried his rib was broken.

Feeling inspired, Cole spun his ax around to ward off Falor and Pete-Pete's advance. He thrashed wildly at the two henchmen and backed them into a corner in the alley. Falor ducked under a wild swing and Cole's ax got stuck between stones in a wall.

Falor shouted, "Ha!" which gave Cole enough time to wrench his ax out of the wall. A few stones came with it and one hit Falor's head, knocking him unconscious.

Pal whistled. Pete-Pete turned, and Pal made two cuts at Pete-Pete's waist, holstering his daggers.

Pete-Pete chuckled and said, "You missed. You missed." He took a step forward and realized Pal didn't miss. Pete-Pete's belt fell in four pieces. His pants dropped to his ankles and revealed his stained underwear. Pete-Pete blushed.

Pal crouched, executed a perfect backflip, and kicked Pete-Pete's chin. The shockwave of pain knocked him out cold.

Markos threw a few well-placed punches into Cole's ribs. A frightened raccoon, who had been feasting on rubbish, bleated when the large human nearly fell on him. Cole grabbed the raccoon by the scruff and tossed it at Markos. The poor raccoon flew, howling through the air, and landed on Marko's face. It frantically clawed its way to the top of his head.

Falor dragged Pete-Pete out of the alley and Markos followed, sobbing like a baby.

Seconds after the fight was over, Cole shouted, "That was awesome!"

"We have to get out of here," Pal said.

"He was like grrrr. And I was like raaah!" Cole said and grabbed his stomach in pain. He found a liquid rose in his palm.

"Are you alright?" Pal asked.

The excitement of battle hid the pain. Now over, Cole was aware of his injury.

"Tis but a scratch," Cole said.

"Well, it was a poison dagger, so..."

As if on cue, Cole turned white and fell unconscious. Pal stared down at the large blond drunken idiot at his feet. Why did he help him? Did he pity the big galoot? If he did, was it even worth it to anger Sarik?

For a second Pal considered leaving. But when he looked at Cole, who was turning more ghostly pale by the second, he couldn't. Perhaps deep within Pal's corrupt heart, there was a sliver of unselfishness.

Pal slipped his hands under Cole's armpits and dragged his heavy body into the moonlit street. He was greeted by the tip of Hikari's katana.

"Murderer."

"I know how it looks, but I'm actually trying to save him," Pal said.

"And a liar. How will the gods sentence you in the court of heaven?"

"Our friend will be in the court of heaven soon if we don't get him some help."

"What have you done?" Hikari asked.

"Me?" Pal said. "Nothing. But the guys who attacked us poisoned him. Most likely with a scorpion dagger. If we don't get him to a healer soon, he's as good as dead."

Hikari lowered his sword.

CHAPTER NINE

The Glue

The next morning in a modest room of an inn, Cole lay in bed, drenched in his own sweat. The sun shone through the window and its warmth woke him. He mumbled a few incoherent sentences and grimaced. As his vision returned, Pal came into focus. He sat in a chair at the side of the bed. His eyes had the weary look of someone who had not slept the entire night.

"Feeling better?" Pal asked.

"I feel like I got stabbed."

"You did," Pal said with a hint of a smile.

Cole grunted and pulled the covers up around his neck. He wasn't sure what hurt more, his wound or his headache.

The door opened and Hikari entered the room with a bowl of water. "Good. You're awake," he said and placed the bowl on a table near the window.

Sunlight reflected off the paladin's golden chainmail armor. Cole shielded his eyes from the glare. "Not him again," Cole said, hoisted himself up, and groaned as a searing pain shot across his abdomen.

"You must rest," Hikari said.

Cole waved him away. "I'm fine," he said and stood, took a step, and fell flat on his face. Hikari rushed to his side. "I said, I'm fine."

Cole stood unassisted. He walked to the table near the window, dipped his hands into the bowl and splashed water on his face. It was cool and invigorating, so he took another handful and washed his neck and hair.

Hikari announced with pride, "By the power of Rey, I have healed you."

Cole thanked him without ceremony and sat on the edge of the bed.

"Tell me, Cole, do you know why those men tried to kill you?" Hikari asked, his eyes fixed on Pal.

Pal said, "There was an argument at the bar. It spilled onto the street."

"They started it!" Cole exclaimed and then grabbed his side, wincing.

Hikari returned his attention to Cole and said, "The men who attacked you were gang members. Very dangerous and prevalent in these parts. You're lucky you survived."

Cole grinned from ear to ear. "Luck had nothing to do with it. With Death's Edge in my hand, I could conquer an entire army. Why don't we hunt down the rest of those twerps and make them pay for their crimes?"

"And what of your quest to rescue the princess?" Hikari asked.

"Forget her. Harold, the king's ambassador, bailed on me. He was my ticket to meet the king."

"Ah, yes," Hikari recalled. "I heard about him. The town crier announced his body washed up on shore this morning. Mugged and stabbed."

Cole snapped his fingers. "That's why he didn't show. He didn't stand me up. He was dead."

"Good excuse," Pal said.

Cole clapped his hands and rubbed them together. "Harold must not have died in vain. The quest is back on. We save the princess, return her to the king, collect our reward, and on to the next adventure."

"Excuse me," Pal said. "Did you say reward?"

"Sure," Cole said. "There's a big reward. I don't know how much, but..."

"A hundred pounds of silver," Hikari said.

"A hundred pounds of silver?" Cole and Pal asked in unison.

"Yes. The town crier is a terrible gossip. I was able to retrieve most of my information from him, although I had to wade through a lake's worth of rumors and scandals." Hikari shook his head. He was not the least bit interested in the latest scandals of the royal class. "Cole, we must seek an audience with his majesty at once."

"Agreed." Cole stood carefully, testing his balance. "What are we waiting for? Let's go."

"Not all of us are invited," Hikari said.

"Hey! Why can't I come?" Cole asked.

"Not you Cole. He means me," Pal said.

"Why not?" Cole asked Hikari. "We need Pal."

"I do not think it is a good idea," Hikari whispered.

"But Pal is great in a pinch. He does this thing with his daggers..." Cole twirled imaginary daggers and threw them wildly across the room like a child entertaining his parents. "And he can talk his way out of tough situations. And he's got style. I mean, look at his outfit. It's way better than mine."

Hikari looked the man in black up and down and said, "He is a rogue."

"Actually, I'm a locksmith. Not to say that I haven't had my run-ins with the law but those days are long behind me. I'm an honest man working in an honest trade now," Pal said, appealing to Cole's naivete.

"See, Hikari?"

Hikari narrowed his eyes. "I don't trust him."

Pal shrugged and said, "Who can you trust in this world?"

Frowning, Cole crossed his arms. "I'm not going unless Pal comes too," he said.

After a moment of reflection, Hikari reluctantly agreed. Cole pumped his fist in the air and hooted, "Great! We're an adventuring party! One paladin, one locksmith, and me the leader!"

Hikari looked at his feet. He was too polite to nominate himself but didn't feel comfortable with a novice leading the group. Pal picked up on it and jumped at the opportunity to gain the paladin's trust.

"No offense Cole, but how are you the leader? Don't get me wrong, I don't like this guy," Pal said and thrust his thumb in Hikari's direction, "but he is a paladin. He's more powerful than you and me combined. Plus, anyone who sees him will think he's in charge. That makes him top dog."

"Yeah, but," Cole stammered, "I brought us together."

Pal's hazel eyes brightened and a sly smile crept up the corner of his mouth. "You know what, Cole? Maybe you're not the leader. Maybe you're the glue."

"The glue?"

"Yeah. The leader makes final decisions for the party, but the glue...," Pal said and paused for effect, "...the glue keeps us all together."

"The glue," Cole said and nodded. "I like that. Alright. I'm the glue. Let's grab our gear and get going. I mean, if that's okay with you Hikari."

"By all means," Hikari said.

Cole grabbed his ax and said, "Come on Death's Edge, adventure awaits us," and ran out the door. A second later, he returned, grabbing his boots. He exhaled an embarrassed laugh, stepped into them, and left Hikari and Pal alone. They stared each other down, an epic battle in silence, eyeballing each other to the nth degree.

A deadly serious expression on his face, Hikari said, "I'll be watching you, Pal."

"Lucky for you, I'm pretty," Pal said, puckered up, and blew Hikari a kiss as he left the room. It took all Hikari's willpower not to draw his sword and smite the arrogant silver tongued devil.

CHAPTER TEN

King Langsley

Our party of adventurers—one paladin, one locksmith, and one Cole—arrived at the gothic castle of King Langsley by twilight. Hikari observed the castle's lack of upkeep. The limestone walls, once a clean grayish white, were stained with moss and dirt. In Hikari's homeland, no nobleman—let alone king—would allow their castle to fall into such a state. But customs were different in Redlund, something he reminded himself daily. Pal observed the number of guards patrolling the bastions above. He counted five two-man teams, and two guards standing outside the portcullis below. The wall would be easy to scale, especially since the patrolling guards didn't seem to take their job as seriously as they should. He saw a few dozing, leaning on their pikes to keep from falling down. Cole couldn't believe the size of the castle. He'd never seen a structure of such magnitude. Even the tallest buildings in Flounder dwarfed in comparison. He looked at Hikari, eyes brimming with excitement, but all he could think to say was, "Wow! It's ginormous!"

One of the castle guards woke from their daydream, caught off guard by Cole's voice from below. He rallied the other guards. They spun, drew their weapons, and manned their stations on the wall. They wore plate-mail armor over drab white undergarments and knee-high black leather boots. The

Langsley coat of arms, a silver shooting star, adorned the center of their breastplates. Armed with spears and carrying heavy shields, some of the guards wore egg-shaped helmets. Others donned chainmail hoods. None of the guards were in particularly good physical condition. Cole thought many of them looked like armored pears.

A mustachioed guard wearing a red cape, stationed behind the portcullis pointed his spear and shouted at the party in a self-important tone, "State your business!"

Hikari opened his mouth, but before he got a word out, Cole stepped forward and said, "I am Cole. Cole... of Flounder, and these are my friends. I mean teammates. Well, they are also my friends, but that's beside the point." He cleared his throat. "Long story short, the reason we are here is to save your princess!"

The guard looked quizzically at Cole.

"Good speech," Pal said sarcastically.

Cole misinterpreted their confusion as a cue for him to extrapolate. "Your Princess...um...Princess, um..."

"Oriel," Hikari said, reminding him as he pinched the bridge of his nose.

"Right. Your Princess Oriel will finally be rescued...by us." Cole said.

He let the message sink in, and when it did, the guards erupted with laughter. A small flame of rage ignited in Cole. *Don't laugh at me*, he thought. The war drums in his ears beat quietly.

Hikari rested a firm, calming hand on Cole's shoulder and stepped in front of him. "I am Hikari Musha, paladin of the sun god Rey."

The laughter morphed into impressed murmurings. "A paladin?! I've never seen one before." "I thought they were all dead." "That's sorcerers, you moron."

The mustachioed guard shouted at the guards above to shut their traps and they quieted. He cocked his head to the side and his egg-shaped helmet shifted with him. "You're a paladin?"

"I am."

"Prove it," the guard said, not in a nasty tone, more out of curiosity.

At first, Hikari didn't react. But then, in the blink of an eye, he drew his glimmering katana, the Sun Sword, and held it above his head. A beacon, Hikari used the katana to channel the power of his god. Sparks of holy light burst off the blade, celestial fireworks. A hum of energy vibrated from the divine instrument. Glittering flakes of sun melted the grass it fell upon.

Cole gasped in absolute wonder. He'd heard tales of how powerful paladins were, but the stories never captured the cleansing sensation and reassuring warmth that overtakes you when standing beside one. There was no more fear, no more anger in Cole, only a captivating sense of awe.

Hikari bellowed, "Not only am I a paladin, but I have no cleric!"

An enormous burst of light exploded off Hikari's blade, sending the guards into a panic. The light glittered and faded until it and the celestial sense of calm it inspired in Cole was gone. The guards peeked from their hiding places behind the wall. They feared fallen paladin. Without a master cleric to serve, they could be bought and were untrustworthy.

Hikari sheathed his sword and returned to his elegant, formal attitude. "My friends and I have been traveling all day. May we be granted an audience with his majesty?"

The mustachioed guard stood at attention. "Yes, yes, of course. Forgive me for wasting your time. I'll bring you to the king myself," the mustachioed guard sputtered. "Raise the portcullis!"

Pal leaned closer to Cole and said, "That's why he's the leader and you're the glue."

Cole sighed, realizing how fruitless it was to compete with Hikari. He thought, *if I can't compete with him, I better learn from him.*

A horn was blown, and within the wall a guard flipped a lever and the portcullis slowly began to rise. An old hunk of junk, it screeched as chains ground against rusty wheels. Hikari and Pal covered their ears, but not Cole, who was too excited to enter his first castle!

The mustachioed guard, whose name they learned was Ward, ushered the party into the keep. He led Cole, Hikari, and Pal through an expansive courtyard. Most guards neglected their stations and engaged in conversation. A few sharpened their swords on whetstones. Some gossiped by the stables.

White flags of shooting stars flew above the quadrangular tower at half-staff, as they have flown since the princess went missing. A steel threaded wooden door opened at Ward's request and the guard entered.

Hikari turned to Pal and said, "Wait here."

Pal spat, and leaned against the stone walls of the keep. He flipped up his hood, crossed his arms, and looked cooler than a glacier. Young house servants passed by, carrying vegetables, fruits, meats, cheeses, and other foods. Some of the girls cast flirtatious glances Pal's way. He replied with a disarming fishhook grin that made them drop their groceries. The castle guards who unsuccessfully flirted with the kitchen staff shot disdainful looks at Pal.

The candlelit hall of the keep was adorned with white banners hanging from a high ceiling. Cole, Hikari, and Ward's footsteps echoed as they crossed the marble floor. Courtiers dressed in pastel tunics and gowns watched from the sidelines.

King Langsley was an ancient, fair-skinned man with a long white beard. He wore a thick, crimson-bear fur with a fluffy white collar and sat on his throne. On his lap, he stroked his scepter like a silver cat. Beside him sat an empty throne.

Ward rushed to the king's adviser and whispered something in his ear, a message the adviser whispered to the King, who nodded and whispered a message his adviser. He delivered the message to the Court Herald, who in turn went through the formalities of announcing the King.

"All hail King Langsley, a king unlike any other king before him or will ever be after him, the wise and wonderful father of all the lands south of Heaven's Peak. A being of such greatness, no words could describe him efficiently. No painter could capture his essence well enough to even bother touching a brush to canvas. No minstrel could sing a melody so sweet to encapsulate his essence. He is our one and only King, chosen by Lord Rey himself. Ruler of all Redlund, from the Endless Forest to the Tranquil Sea. An angel sent from heaven. I present the one and only, King Langsley."

An abrupt fanfare of horns startled Cole. He whispered to Hikari, "Jeez, I thought you had a lot of titles."

Hikari shushed Cole and they approached the throne. Cole smiled and waved at the courtiers in attendance. They responded with unfriendly eyes.

Hikari knelt and said, "Your majesty."

Cole was still in awe, taking in the surroundings. He couldn't believe how many candles the place had. Hikari pulled him down to his knees, and Cole did his best to look like he bowed with as much respect as Hikari.

King Langsley replied in a regal voice, "The fallen paladin, Hikari Musha, I presume?"

Hikari nodded.

King Langsley said, "And your companion?"

"My name is Cole, sir. I mean, your majesty."

"Rise," the King said and they did. "So you have come to rescue my daughter, the Princess Oriel?"

"We have," Hikari said.

"Tell me," King Langsley said. "Why would you go on such a foolhardy mission?"

"I beg your pardon?" Cole asked.

"My daughter went missing over forty years ago. I have given up hope she is still alive. You two put me in a precarious situation. If I turn you away, I appear cruel and heartless. If I send you on this quest, you may never return. Or you might return with any middle-aged maiden you find. After all these years, an old man like me, how would I be able to tell the difference?"

"We'd never do that!"

Hikari glared at Cole, but he didn't notice.

"Look, buddy," Cole said. "If you don't want us to save your daughter, fine. Let's get out of here, Hikari."

The court was aghast. No one spoke that way to the king.

Cole stood, Hikari yanked him back down to the ground, and pleaded with the king. "Pardon my companion, majesty. He is passionate and speaks out of turn."

"Like heck, I do! I didn't come all the way across the sea just to be sent away by some crummy old king."

King Langsley's personal bodyguards drew their swords and advanced. But King Langsley raised his hand and said, "You do not have much experience with kings, do you?"

"You're the first king I've ever met. I thought you'd be a little more..."

"Benevolent? Magnanimous? Altruistic?"

"I was going to say, nice."

"I hate to break it to you, Cole, but *nice* is not a word in a king's vocabulary."

Hikari stood, bowed respectfully. "Thank you for your time, your majesty. We will take our leave now."

Ward led Cole and Hikari to the door.

It wasn't fair. It wasn't right. It wasn't how Cole imagined it at all. The disillusionment stole the last bit of courtesy from him. He felt as if he would explode if he didn't say something.

Cole turned and said, "You know, if she was my daughter, I wouldn't care how many years she was missing. I'd think there was a chance, no matter how slim, she may be alive. And I wouldn't rest until I knew."

The keep's wooden doors flew open. Ward hurried out Hikari and Cole. He was ashamed for bringing the two ignoble guests before the king. It would surely mean a demotion or worse. Ward prayed for demotion.

No one in the court dared speak. They had never seen their king spoken to with such disrespect and had no idea how to return to courtly matters. Neither did King Langsley. Speechless, his eyes fixed on the empty throne beside him.

In the courtyard, Pal whispered a sonnet into a dark-skinned and rather busty servant girl's ear. Mid-stanza, he noticed Cole and Hikari rushing out of the castle. He abandoned his flirtation and gave the girl a wink. She swooned and Pal caught up with his arguing colleagues.

"How'd it go?" Pal asked.

Neither acknowledged him.

"That is not the way you act in front of a King," Hikari told Cole.

"That bad?" Pal asked.

"I don't care," Cole said. "He was rude to us."

Hikari wheeled around on Cole. "Kings are always treated with the utmost respect, regardless of your personal opinion."

"All I'm saying is he's a jerk."

Hikari lost all color in his face.

"He was!" Cole repeated.

"Um, Cole," Pal said and pointed over Cole's shoulder.

Cole turned and met eyes with King Langsley.

"You are right," the King said. "My wife died bringing my daughter into this world. Sixteen years later, my darling Oriel was taken from me too. And forty lonely years have made me stubborn and suspicious. I do not know what my wife would say if she were here today."

"She'd probably say, stop being such a jerk and let these guys help you," Cole said.

Hikari slapped his forehead. Pal smirked. He genuinely liked the kid.

King Langsley smiled remorsefully. "You are passionate, young Cole. Come, I shall tell you all I know concerning my daughter's disappearance. Perhaps your brash attitude is what this old king needs to thaw his frigid heart."

CHAPTER ELEVEN

Negotiations

That night, King Langsley treated Cole, Pal, and Hikari to a feast like they had never known before. The dining hall was lit by a glimmering chandelier of a hundred candles. Portraits of dead Langsleys decorated the walls. Servants brought out course after course of the feast. The mixed aromas of cooked meat, roasted vegetables, hot soups, and other delicacies made Cole's stomach grumble. He reached for a bread roll but Hikari slapped his hand. They were to wait until served.

Rhonda, the servant who caught Pal's attention outside the keep, tied her curly black hair up to show off her long cocoa neck. She seemed to waltz around the table as she served. She locked coquettish eyes with Pal from time to time, which didn't escape Hikari. He worried Pal's open flirtation with the servant would displease the king.

"What can you tell us of the missing princess?" Hikari asked King Langsley.

"Forty years ago, my daughter left for her morning riding lessons. She was a precocious young thing, always straying too far from her instructor. I warned her not to, but she would not listen. Too much of her old man in her," the king said, chuckled and sighed, jogged by a cruel memory. "All they ever found was the horse carcass torn to shreds, and an emerald scale as big as my hand. My royal adviser believes it came from a dragon."

King Langsley snapped his fingers at an adolescent attendant holding a tray of fragrant cheeses. The boy gave them to another servant and rushed out of the room.

"A dragon?" Cole could barely contain his excitement.

Deadly serious, Hikari said, "Dragons are extremely dangerous creatures, your majesty. Are there no other monsters in these parts? Perhaps kobolds or lizard-men?"

"Goblins stalk our woods, but a creature that would shed a scale of this size, I think not," the king replied. "Centuries ago, a fledgling green dragon nested in these parts. It used an evil magic to conceal itself from my great grandfathers and bided its time until it aged and grew large enough to attack. It decimated the kingdom annually. It stole our treasures and ate our livestock until it had its fill and disappeared to its secret lair within the Endless Forest to hibernate. The people of Redlund took to calling the dragon the Emerald Enormity.

"Those days," King Langsley said, motioning to the many portraits in the room. "Life expectancy was twenty years at most. That is why so many kings and queens have sat on the throne before me."

One portrait caught Cole's eye.

"Is that Princess Oriel?"

"Aye," the king said. "She was beautiful. Her mother's looks, of course."

"You got that right," Cole said.

Hikari kicked Cole's leg under the table.

"Ow! What'd I say?"

The doors opened and the young boy returned with a covered silver platter. He set it before the king.

"Thank you," King Langsley said and waved the boy away. "The Emerald Enormity terrorized my land for centuries, disappeared, and never returned."

King Langsley lifted the lid of the silver platter. A large emerald scale rested at its center. Half a foot long and slightly curved; to Cole it was an abominable husk. A faint acidic stench, more potent than vinegar, rose from the dragon scale. Candlelight caught the scale and it cast a greenish hue on the king's beard.

"I believe the Emerald Enormity grew tired of pillaging my kingdom. Our wealth and power grew limited after the many raids we suffered. Our gold and gemstone mines were depleted, one of the many reasons we now deal exclusively in silver, and our farms too meager for a drake's appetite. The dragon may have moved to another country. More likely, it found a way to the Elfwood, home of the elves and other races of the Fair Folk. That is where I suspect the monster resides, plundering elven treasures and pillaging their rich kingdoms."

"So why would the dragon come back?" Cole asked. "Why would he steal your daughter? Don't get me wrong, she's pretty. I mean, she's gorgeous. Stunning actually. Ow! Stop kicking me, Hikari!"

"The truth is, I do not know why she was abducted or if it even was the dragon. It could have been coincidence my men found the scale at the site of her disappearance. We will never know for certain since all who witnessed her kidnapping were slaughtered. All I knew was I had to act upon a worst case scenario.

"At first, I assumed if it was the Emerald Enormity it was obvious the dragon desired a ransom. I pooled as much of the treasury as I could without bankrupting the kingdom, and sent a rescue party into the Endless Forest. My men wandered the woods in search of the dragon. If they found it, I shall never know. Not a single man returned."

"And the treasure?" Pal asked.

"Gone with the men. I sent ambassadors to every corner of Eld in search of heroes to rescue my daughter and retrieve our treasure. Many brave men went into the forest. None came back. As the years dragged on, interest in the quest declined, and eventually, brave men stopped coming.

"More years passed and then I began to forget her. First, it was her voice. I could not remember how she sounded. Next, it was the features of her face. One by one, those qualities that made her unique, that made her *my* daughter began to disappear. Now, my only memory of her is the painting on the wall. I have stared at that painting every day since she was taken from me. It is the only image of her I have anymore. My memory of her is as dry as the paint on the canvas."

King Langsley's lip quivered. Tears wet his eyes. He lowered his head and swallowed hard several times. "Excuse me," he said and raised a napkin to cover his lips.

Hikari reached out and took the king's hand. Warm divine energy passed through their touch. "Sometimes the mind forgets what the heart knows," Hikari said.

King Langsley looked into the paladin's reassuring eyes, a gaze no courtier dared for fear of disrespecting him. But the King was still a man and all men need comfort. He smiled at Hikari. Feeling exonerated, he took a refreshing breath and straightened his posture. "You must seek out the gate."

"What gate?" Cole asked.

"The gate to Elfwood. It is rarely opened these days. Our alliance with the elves is hardly congenial. They blame humans for any and all problems with the environment. It is why they lock themselves in their own realm and refuse to trade their resources. Their embargo has crippled our economy for decades." The king scowled and lifted his goblet. "Stubborn creatures are the elves."

Roderick, the butler, rang a bell. The servants in attendance rushed in to distract King Langsley from a foul mood. They served dishes of roasted hen, steamed mixed greens, baked potatoes, and fresh loaves of hearty bread. Cole had never attended a king's feast and did not know when to begin. Hikari waited for King Langsley to take the first bite, but Cole beat him to it, sucking on a tender drumstick and slathering his steaming potato with butter.

"The boy does not understand etiquette, does he?" King Langsley asked Hikari.

"He means well."

Cole belched and bit off the heel off a loaf of bread.

Rhonda refilled Pal's glass and whispered something in his ear before heading back into the kitchen with the other servants. Pal watched her leave but addressed the table. "Excuse me, but goblins, elves, and dragons? This mission is getting more dangerous by the second."

"Pal is correct. To defeat a dragon, we will need wisdom from those who have defeated dragons before. We must consult the elves," Hikari said.

"Curse the elves," King Langsley said. "They have made it clear they wish to have no communication with humans."

"They would not turn away a paladin."

"Forgive my saying so, but Hikari, you are a fallen paladin. And a human. The elves may not accept you as readily as I," King Langsley said.

"Of course you're right, majesty, but..." Pal slurped from his glass to guarantee the spotlight was his, "what I've been driving at is the price. Sure, we're prepared to risk our lives to bring your precious princess home, even if we have to slay an entire fleet of dragons. The thing is, a job this dangerous, if we succeed and survive, we should be properly compensated."

"And what would you consider proper?" King Langsley asked in clipped tones.

"The reward is currently one hundred pounds of silver, but what year was that reward established? Thirty, forty years ago?"

King Langsley groaned exasperation. "What are you driving at?"

Pal shrugged. "We have to account for inflation."

King Langsley narrowed his eyes and growled, "The entire kingdom is in a great depression."

"And we are about to brighten its spirits with the return of their missing princess," Pal said with a smirk. "So I imagine the reward should be higher."

"Exactly how much higher were you imagining?" King Langsley asked.

"Two hundred," Pal said.

"Two hundred?! Outrageous!" King Langsley exclaimed and turned to Cole. "I thought you were here to help me, not extort me!"

"Don't look at me," Cole said with a mouthful of hen. "He's the businessman. I'm just the glue."

Pal stood and threw his napkin on the table. "If two hundred pounds of silver are worth more to you than your daughter, we thank you for the lovely dinner and we'll be on our way. Come on, Cole."

"Two hundred pounds of silver," King Langsley reeled, exasperated. "You'd never be able to carry it."

Pal clapped Cole on the shoulders and said, "He's stronger than he looks."

Cole was moved by the compliment. He took a few extra bites from his plate, grabbed a dinner roll for the road, and stood. "I'm sorry, King Langsley. I really wanted to save your daughter. Let's go, Hikari."

Hikari was frozen in shock by Pal's abhorrent behavior. Before he could formulate a sentence, King Langsley stood and shouted, "Wait! I will pay."

Cole looked into Pal's eyes. They sparkled with triumph, but he still managed to keep his signature cool demeanor. Pal winked at Cole and they returned to the table.

"Glad you've come around to see things our way. It would be a shame for this entire quest to fall apart before it even began," Pal said.

Cole agreed with that full heartedly.

King Langsley leaned back in his chair and sighed. "The silver will take some time to gather," he said.

"We understand. Now, will the silver come in tabs or circs? Circs are obviously preferred since they're easier to break but tabs are suitable. As long as the silver is real, we're fine. Slips are a no go," Pal leaned over to Cole, "an I.O.U. is about as welcome in most Langsley shops as a touch of the plague."

"I'll have the silver for you in circs."

"Great. That's great. And don't worry. We'll be back with your daughter in the blink of an eye," Pal reassured him. "Now about that advance..."

"Advance?!"

"We will need some money for supplies for our journey."

King Langsley paused, his anger palpable.

"Roderick."

The butler stepped forward and bowed. "Your highness?"

"See to it these men are well situated for their journey."

"Yes, majesty."

Roderick bowed and hurried off.

Under the table, Pal nudged Cole with his foot. They smiled at each other. Their exclusive little club annoyed Hikari.

"You are most generous," the paladin said and bowed.

Pal stood and bowed with a flourish to the king. Out the corner of his eye, Pal saw Rhonda peeking from behind a door. She flashed a seductive smile and closed the door.

Pal stretched and said, "Now that negotiation is over, I need to use the privy. Excuse me."

"But you haven't touched your dinner," Cole said with a mouthful of food.

"I have other appetites," Pal whispered as he slid his plate in front of Cole.

Cole smiled, stabbed his fork into a baked potato, took a huge bite, and chewed with his mouth open.

King Langsley contemplated the price he agreed to pay as he sipped his grog.

CHAPTER TWELVE

Double Dealing

Castle Langsley was a thief's dream. Treasures were mere decorations. Paintings and tapestries lined the walls. Woven rugs with intricate patterns ran the hallway floors. And the silver, oh, how the silver gleamed. Pal desired it all. Precious metals called to him the way a harp calls to its minstrel, both needing to be stroked and adored. He caressed a heavy candlestick perched on a shelf. It was softer than brass and heavier too. Perfection.

Pal licked his lips and glanced over his shoulder. *No one will miss one silver candlestick*, he convinced himself. He blew out the candle, and wrapped his greedy fingers around it.

"What do you think you're doing?"

Pal froze. He didn't hear anyone approach. Unusual for him, since he was always on high alert. He turned and saw Rhonda standing at the end of the hallway then relaxed and smiled. She cat walked up to him, applying red stain to her lips.

Pal said, "I was admiring the..."

She grabbed him by the collar and pulled him an inch away from her lips.

"Direct. I like that," Pal said and leaned in for a kiss, but got kneed in the groin instead. He buckled and fell, clutching himself in agony.

"What was that for?" Pal asked.

Rhonda's demeanor shifted. Her gentle flirtatious attitude turned hard as granite. She lowered her plump red stained lips to his and kissed him. It was long and slow and ugly, smashing her lips against his until Pal couldn't breathe.

After she released him and he replenished his lungs with oxygen, he asked, "Who do you work for?"

Rhonda whispered in his ear, "You're speaking too loud. Whispers are not meant to be heard..."

Pal completed her sentence. "They're meant to be a secret." He opened his shirt and revealed a tattoo of the letter F. Between the F's arm and tie, was an eye spying through a keyhole.

"You don't deserve to wear that," Rhonda spat.

"What's this about Sarik?" Pal said looking past her.

Pal and Sarik shared a long history together. Not because they liked each other—both men considered the other a friend of convenience—but saving one another's hides countless times did create a bond between them. It was Pal who encouraged Sarik to form the Locksmiths. Establishing a new gang in Redlund would focus an unwanted spotlight on them, but organizing a group of thieves under the front of a locksmith guild was devious and fail-safe. They already had the skills necessary to pose as a locksmith and they needed a cover story for all the suspicious equipment they carried. Most important, The Locksmiths organization offered its members unity. Unity meant strength and protection. Disloyalty meant death, and tonight Sarik was determined to carry out Pal's sentence.

Earlier, at sundown, Sarik had infiltrated the castle unnoticed. He eliminated unsuspecting guards along the way, and with Rhonda's help, found a secret passage to the dining room. There he watched Pal (the treacherous weasel) feast with the king.

After dinner, Sarik crept along the dark passages hidden behind the castle walls. He followed Pal to the hallway where he met Rhonda. The kiss was a perfect distraction. Rhonda belonged to Sarik, but he didn't mind using her to seduce weaker men for his benefit. He'd entered the hallway through a secret entrance behind a display of standing armor. "You're not as dumb as you act," Sarik said, drawing daggers from his belt.

"The kid was inebriated," Pal said.

"So you thought you'd save his life?" Sarik asked, disgusted. "You're a Locksmith—a thief!"

His throat unexpectedly dry, Pal swallowed his spit, and said, "You're right. We are thieves. But we are not murderers."

"Don't be so pessimistic," Sarik said. "I may make a murderer of you yet."

"Don't you see what this stupid kid has done for us? Can you not see past him embarrassing you? Look where we're having this conversation. We are in Castle Langsley."

Sarik chewed his bottom lip. He hated to admit it, but Pal was right. Blinded by his ego he didn't realize he had infiltrated the biggest treasure vault in the kingdom. A sinister smirk curled up the side of his mouth. "So all along this was all a plot to get the Locksmiths inside the castle?"

"Yes."

"Goblin dung!" Rhonda exclaimed.

"I wasn't literally trying to get us inside the castle, but since I have I feel as if I am due some thanks."

"Don't push your luck, Pal," Sarik said, pointing a dagger at him. "Your claim is a stretch."

"After word spread that the Blackfeet Boys murdered an ambassador to the King yesterday on the docks, you sent me on a reconnaissance mission. Contrary to your suspicions, there was no intel on any upcoming war. I knew we could rest assured that the good people of Redlund would keep their money at home, right where we want them too. But digging a little deeper, I discovered the ambassador brought a new hero from across the sea to rescue the princess. The one who's been missing for forty years. I also learned they were going to meet at the Drunken Skeleton."

"Yeah yeah, and the hero never showed," Sarik interrupted. "I know all that. I was there."

"You're wrong, Sarik. He did show. Cole, the dumb kid from the Drunken Skeleton, he is the hero."

Sarik laughed. "The fool who drenched me in grog?" he asked and laughed again. Rhonda joined him.

"It's true," Pal said, wiping sweat from his forehead. He felt dizzy and his muscles and joints burned.

"Fine. The old tyrant Langsley wants to ship another hero off to his death on a fool's errand. I buy that, but the other guy? Uh-uh. Who's the paladin?" Sarik sneered.

"Hikari Musha. He is Cole's connection. They met yesterday and hit it off, but it's not like they've got history. Not like you and me, at least. Cole tells him about the princess and you know how paladins are, they can't help but join a quest. I'm telling you Sarik, this kid seems like a total moron, but there's something about him. I don't think we should underestimate him."

"We? There is no we anymore."

"Sarik, I'm sorry," Pal said before he doubled over and heaved a few dry painful coughs. Hot flashes pulsing through his body turned to icy tremors.

Sarik moved closer to Pal, placed the flat end of one of his daggers under Pal's chin, lifting it so they made eye contact. "Trust is everything my friend," Sarik said. "And frankly, I just don't trust you anymore."

"What have you done to me?"

Sarik smiled and crow's feet appeared around his dark sinister eyes. "You have been infected with a slow acting poison." He glanced at Rhonda, who reapplied her poison lip stain and then turned back to Pal. "It is fatal, but lucky for you, I have the antidote."

Pal gasped and wretched. His tongue swelled and he collapsed on the ground. Sarik could have killed him right there but like most evil people, he enjoyed toying with his victims more than administering a quick death.

"Don't be such a wuss," Rhonda said. She fluffed her thick curly hair and admired her reflection on a polished suit of armor. "The dry mouth will pass and the pain will move into your chest." Rhonda crossed to Sarik and draped herself on him. "Soon it will pass into your intestines. That is when the real pain begins," she concluded with a horrible giggle.

"What do you want from me?" Pal asked.

"Since you've agreed to go on this foolhardy quest to save the princess, if you're lucky enough to make it back alive, I want the reward," Sarik said.

Wheezing on the floor, Pal said, "Fifty percent."

Rhonda stepped on Pal's Adam's apple. He let out a deep guttural click. He was too weak to lift her foot. It was impossible.

"You're in no position to negotiate," she said.

"I have something you want," Pal said with effort, "And you have something I want. That is a perfect place to start negotiations."

Rhonda looked to Sarik. He waved her away and she lifted her heel. Pal guzzled oxygen.

"Tell me, Pal, do you want to live or not?" Sarik asked.

"I do. But why should I do all the legwork? Fifty percent."

"Ninety," Sarik fired back.

"Seventy-five."

"Eighty."

"Deal," Pal said and offered his weak hand.

Sarik did not take it. "I'll need to think about it. Wait by the window in your bedchamber tonight. If I accept your deal of eighty percent of the reward, I'll deliver you the antidote."

"If not?"

"You won't make it through the night," Rhonda said and pricked his neck with a concealed needle. "That should keep you from choking on your own tongue until midnight. Better pray Sarik has made up his mind by then."

Pal felt instant relief, his breathing steadied and his tongue shrank, but he glared at Rhonda.

"It's all about trust," Sarik said. "As long as I feel like I can trust you, I want you on my side."

"But you can never trust a thief," Pal said, pushing himself up off the floor.

"You may not be able to trust a thief, but in the end, you can always count on someone to choose the biggest payday." Sarik and Rhonda slunk into the secret passage behind the display of armor. He pulled a hidden lever and the standing display of armor slid back in place covering the secret passage.

Cole bounded into the hallway. "Pal, where have you been?"

"In the privy," Pal said. "Have you seen this place? It's big enough to get lost in."

"I know. A real castle. My dream come true." Cole was so excited he danced on his toes.

"What did I miss?" Pal asked.

"Right. The mission. It's on. Good work with the negotiations. Two hundred pounds of silver is a fortune. I'm going to be rich enough to buy a real suit of armor and pay back my old roommates Jerome and Dante. I knew bringing you on the team was a good idea."

Cole clapped Pal on the back. In his weak condition, Pal felt as if he had been hit with a war hammer, but concealed his pain, and Cole was none the wiser.

The pair walked to their bedchamber. Cole, in his excitement, led the way, explaining the details of the quest. Pal lagged behind, leaning against the walls to stay on his feet.

"We leave tomorrow morning," Cole said. "I can't wait."

"Better get some sleep. You're going to need it."

"I don't think I'll ever be able to sleep."

Ten minutes later, Cole passed out in their bedchamber, snoring. Hikari slept on a bedroll beside Cole's bed. One hand clutched the hilt of his katana. Pal stood at the window looking out over the courtyard. His eyes heavy and breath scarce, a deadly fever coursed through his veins and he shuddered with chills. Sweat poured down his burning neck and bare back.

Thhhp. Pal snatched an arrow shot into the room out of midair. Although nearly dead, his reflexes were as nimble as a cat's. A vial of clear liquid and a tiny scroll were tied to the arrow. Pal unfurled the parchment and could hear Sarik's gravelly voice as he read:

We may or may not be following you, but we will be watching.

The note disintegrated and its ashes blew out the window.

No turning back, Pal thought as he popped the cork from the vial and greedily drank the antidote.

CHAPTER THIRTEEN

Way of the Warrior

Cole woke the next morning with the rising sun. It had been a great night's sleep. Living with Dante and Jerome, he slept on the floor. Good for his posture, but uncomfortable. He could get used to beds.

Cole looked around the bedchamber and saw Pal was asleep in a plush arm chair and Hikari was gone. He lifted his shirt and checked the knife wound on his belly. He was surprised to see it was nothing more than a scar. He poked it with his finger and felt no pain. *I am stronger than I look,* he thought.

"Psst. Pal? Are you awake?"

"No," Pal grumbled.

"Oh, sorry. Wait a second. You are awake. I still don't get your sense of humor, Pal, but I will. Do you know where Hikari is?"

"Can't talk. Sleeping."

"How are you sleeping if we're having a conversation?"

Pal's eyes flashed open. "You're right Cole. I'm not sleeping because you won't let me sleep. So please, BE QUIET!"

"You're not a morning person, are you? I am, as you can tell. You'll probably be more pleasant in the afternoon."

"Maybe," Pal said and curled into a ball.

"Okay. Well, if you want you can sleep in my bed, it's really comfortable. You should try it."

Pal grunted.

"See you later," Cole said and left the room. A second later he returned. "I forgot Death's Edge." Cole picked up his ax and slung it over his shoulder, but as he turned to leave the room the ax tore into a tapestry. "Oops." He stumbled back a few feet and bumped into a dresser, knocking over a priceless vase. It shattered on the floor. He spun around to pick up the pieces and his ax knocked over an entire tray of goblets, dishes, and silverware. Making an incredible amount of noise, Cole frantically began to clean up.

Pal jumped out of his chair and shouted, "Leave it!"

"I'm sorry. Are you sure I shouldn't clean this up?"

"Just go!"

"You're right. They must have someone who takes care of these kinds of accidents."

"For the love of all that is holy, go!" Pal begged.

Cole cradled his ax, his baby, and carried it out of the room.

Pal exhaled relief.

Cole closed the door and the painting of King Langsley behind the armchair fell onto Pal's head.

Cole strolled through the sunny courtyard, yawned, and scratched his itchy rear. Castle guards went about their daily business. He smiled to himself. He finally made it. He was a real adventurer in a real castle with real guards!

Cole found Hikari practicing his sword work in the center of the courtyard. He trained with unerring discipline, an ancient progression of paladin swordplay. Cole joined a small crowd who came to watch the paladin. Hikari wielded the Sun Sword with delicacy and deadly precision. With each varied attack, he left a trace of light in its wake.

After Hikari completed his morning routine, Cole and the crowd applauded. Once they dispersed, Cole approached Hikari and said, "That was incredible. What are you doing?"

"Training."

"But I thought you're a master."

Hikari sheathed his sword. "Even masters train. Care to join?"

"Nah. I'm a natural talent. I don't need training."

"You may be talented, my friend, but talent won't carry you in a fight."

"I did pretty well against those thieves," Cole said.

Hikari's charismatic grin defused Cole's temper. "Thieves are one thing. A dragon is another."

Cole drew his ax and spun the hilt in his hands. "As long as it bleeds, I can kill it," he said and shattered a cobblestone underfoot with Death's Edge.

"You want to be a hero, right?" Hikari asked.

"Right."

"Well, heroes are made, not born. Hard work, training, and living by your ideals, that's what makes a true hero."

"That and a couple of titles," Cole muttered.

"Titles are not as important as accomplishments."

"Easy for you to say, Mr. Squire of our Planet's Star, Guardian of blah blah blah. Me? I'm nothing. Just Cole the orphan."

Hikari sighed, gazed east towards the rising sun, and said, "I was headstrong like you when I was a student. The difference was I had no talent. But I trained daily. As you can see, a warrior with no talent who trains daily can become a master. A natural talent who does not train will never grow. But a natural talent who trains may become the greatest warrior of all."

Sold, Cole agreed to join Hikari in his morning training sessions from that day on.

Hikari and Cole trained until mid-afternoon. They began with basic offensive and defensive techniques to live by. Being a natural talent, Cole improved by the end of the first lesson. His footwork, hand-eye coordination, and strength were all there. What he needed to work on was his main weakness—his temper. Every misstep, every wrong attack, every minuscule mistake sent Cole into a fit of rage. These temper tantrums worried Hikari. His entire approach on the battlefield was based on composed, calculated attacks.

At midday, Pal sauntered up to Cole and Hikari, who were exhausted.

"Ready to get that reward?"

CHAPTER FOURTEEN

The Endless Forest

Cole, Hikari, and Pal entered the dense pine woods of the Endless Forest. Cole felt claustrophobic walking through the narrow spaces separating the trees. His belly scraped against the scaly bark of a tree, tearing a hole in his shirt. He growled and grumbled, cursing at the evergreen and drove Death's Edge into its trunk.

"What's going on back there?" Hikari asked.

"Stupid-gosh-darn-dumb-tree!" Cole mumbled to himself.

Pal couldn't help but chuckle at his companion's overreaction, but Hikari did not find it amusing. An unfamiliar forest was no place to lose one's composure. He decided he would teach Cole a calming prayer when they next stopped to rest.

Again, Cole was overwhelmed by the amount of walking involved in adventure. "How much longer?" he asked Hikari.

"Not long."

Cole groaned, acting like a spoiled child.

Pal stopped dead in his tracks and said, "Do you hear that?"

"I don't hear a thing," Cole said.

Pal shushed him and they paused and listened. Cole only heard the beating of his anxious heart. Hikari's senses were alert, but his stoic demeanor did not betray his alarm. The party took cautious steps deeper into the forest toward whatever it was Pal heard.

Pal led Hikari and Cole into a thicket. Flecks of sunlight shined through the needles, speckling the ground. Even in daylight, Cole was spooked.

"Where are you taking us?" he asked.

"Quiet," Pal said.

The party moved forward. The sound of drums grew from a distant pitter-patter to a resounding thunder. Cole's heart beat to the music. He was nervous and excited all at once, sweat welled out of his forehead and hung from his brow. He wiped it with his forearm, clearing his vision.

Pal crouched and the others imitated him. They made themselves as small and quiet as possible. At this, Pal was superior because of his practice at thievery for many years. Cole wasn't half bad himself and it surprised him how easy sneaking was. It wasn't his style, but he learned more about himself daily and liked picking up new tricks. Hikari was the loudest of the three. His chainmail clinked with each step, so he fell behind the others.

Pal and Cole came to a cluster of bushes, waited for Hikari to arrive, and on Pal's cue, they peeked over a bush. There, in the middle of a clearing in the woods, they discovered a band of...

"Goblins!" Cole exclaimed.

The goblins were tiny reptilian humanoids with wrinkled, flat faces. Two fangs sprouted from their protruding lower lip, like pigs, except they weren't cute at all. Their skin varied a purplish brown or yellowish green. They were scaly and covered with warts and boils. Most wore rags, though some of the larger goblins donned wooden armor. They carried battered morning stars, short swords, clubs, and crossbows. Horned metal skull caps adorned the tops of their small heads.

Around a campfire, the goblins prepared to lunch. They sang a goblin song, a melody composed of high-pitched burps and wet farts. A goblin shaman wearing a tattered robe wielded a cane like a baton. He conducted the song with deranged glee. Behind the shaman was an effigy of a dragon. Made of sticks and moss and held together with dried mud and vines.

Roasting over the fire was a dark skinned man with a thick and unruly fro, his hands and feet bound with rope to the spit. His colorful dashiki dress was licked by the flames. His sandals were bloodied from running. Goblins ransacked his backpack, a bookshelf with straps. The soon to be barbecued man reprimanded the goblins like a frustrated teacher in a schoolroom full of naughty children. "Take that magical tome out of your mouth! And you! Put those potions down! You're breaking invaluable ancient artifacts! Hands off my scrolls! You wouldn't understand them anyway. They are written in Arcana, and as far as I know, goblins are illiterate!"

Cole, Hikari, and Pal ducked behind the bush.

"It's a sorcerer! We have to save him," Cole said, dying for action.

"We need a plan before we attack," Hikari said.

Cole rushed into the clearing.

"Or not," Pal said.

"Hey, you smelly little creeps!" Cole shouted.

The goblins turned, their pointed ears cocked to the side reminded Cole of curious dogs.

"Let him go!" Cole ordered.

The goblins looked at the large pink man with straw-colored hair and a deep frown etched into his brow. And although goblins can't count (at least not like we can), they sensed they outnumbered the human. The goblins cracked up, laughing till their sides hurt.

"Don't laugh at me," Cole said, shaking with rage. The war drums beat in his ears and he raised Death's Edge high above his head. Screaming his signature battle cry, he charged.

Cole plowed through the crowd of shocked goblins right for the shaman. He drove Death's Edge through the shaman's body like a knife cuts warm cheese.

"Wait! Free me first!" the goblin's prisoner exclaimed, looking at the fire kindling below him.

Cole hacked his way through the band of goblins. It took a few more kills before the stupid creatures sensed the danger the pink man presented.

Hikari and Pal entered the fight. Hikari drew the Sun Sword and reflected blinding sunlight into the goblins' eyes. They lifted their tiny arms and clawed hands up to block the glare. This gave Cole enough time to cleave through three goblins' necks. Their heads spun like tops in the air and their bodies collapsed.

Pal dashed over to the fire and freed the prisoner with his dagger. Standing to his full height, the dark skinned man was only five feet tall. His body in immaculate physical condition, every muscle was lean and strong and tight. Pal couldn't tell if his large brown eyes brimmed with supreme intelligence or madness, a common trait for those who dabble in the arcane arts.

The wizard looked up into the eyes of his savior. "You came just in time!" he exclaimed. "I was sure I was going to be a barbecued wizard."

"You owe me." *Never hurts to have a wizard owe you a favor*, Pal thought.

On the battlefield, Cole made mincemeat of the goblins. One goblin, he batted to the ground with the flat edge of his ax. Another, he cut diagonally down his chest.

"Is that all you got?" he shouted.

The little goblin Cole beat to the ground raised his Morningstar and slammed it down on his foot like a hammer. The nail on Cole's big toe, the little piggy that went to market, exploded. He dropped his ax and hopped around, howling in pain. Six goblins rushed over and tackled him.

Covered by goblins, Cole tapped into his deep reservoir of inner strength. Growling, he pushed himself up to his feet. The goblins clung to him, biting, punching, kicking, and pulling his hair. He roared furious gibberish, jumped into the air, and landed on his back. The goblins popped like zits.

Only one goblin survived. Its legs shattered and lungs collapsed, the little bugger crawled out from under Cole, but it didn't make it far. Cole grabbed the goblin's ankle and flung the foul creature into a tree. The goblin's skull cracked and it fell dead.

Hikari stabbed a charging goblin in the chest with the Sun Sword. Beams of light radiated from its open eyes and mouth. Pressure built inside the goblin until it exploded. Goblin bits rained over the paladin and drenched his golden chainmail in blackish green sludge.

Another goblin raised its crossbow and aimed it at Hikari, but a floating ruby distracted it. The goblin dropped his crossbow and chased the ruby as children chase fireflies. The wizard directed the illusionary ruby to float in front of Pal, who promptly stabbed the tiny goblin.

"Nice trick," Pal said.

Two goblins flanking Pal rushed him, their swords thrust forward, and Pal stepped back and they stabbed each other.

"Bravo!" the wizard exclaimed.

Hikari turned on a few goblins sneaking up behind him and took a low defensive stance. The clouds above him parted.

Sunlight illuminated his chainmail. The petrified goblins dropped their weapons and fled screaming.

Pal drew small throwing daggers from secret compartments in his black outfit. He dealt them across the battlefield not missing a single target. "Thirteen, fourteen, fifteen...," he counted.

The wizard opened a spell book and read aloud.

"Rise dragon roots, claws and wings
Haunt these goblins, do foul things."

The dragon effigy began to dance. The remaining goblins were mesmerized by their idol miraculously coming to life. Fireworks screeched out of the exposed ribs of wood, chasing off the last of the goblins.

"And don't come back!" Cole shouted.

Hikari patted Cole on the back and said, "Good work."

"Thanks, Hikari."

"But next time, we make a plan of attack. Heroes always plan before they attack."

"We won didn't we?"

"The only battle you must win is the last battle."

"Yeah, well, I think better on my toes. Ah! My toes!"

Cole removed off his boot. His sock soaked in blood, he whimpered as he peeled it off. His toenail ruptured and his toe was extremely swollen.

Hikari knelt, took Cole's foot in his hand, lowered his head, and prayed. Warm, soothing, divine energy flowed from him into his student. The toenail crackled back into its rightful shape. The toe shrunk to its normal size and the pain evaporated.

Astounded, Cole asked, "How did you do that?"

"Same as when I healed you at the inn, with prayer. Rey provides me with strength and power. All he asks is my loyalty."

"Amazing. Anytime I get hurt, you do your paladin thing and I'm healed?"

"My powers are not unlimited, Cole. I must pray daily to recharge what energies I borrow from the almighty sun. No resource in this world is infinite."

"Sure, sure. I get it. You pray and I'm healed. Easy enough."

"Cole," Hikari said, but the boy was already off.

Pal retrieved his daggers from the felled goblins. Sensing someone watching him, he turned.

The wizard picked up a handful of mud. "You saved my life," he said. "It is the custom of my people that I guard you until I have returned the favor. Upon this mud, I make my bond." He shook Pal's hand and squeezed the warm dark mess between their fingers.

Pal was aghast. "You know that was goblin dung."

The wizard grinned. "Our pact is even more sacred."

Cole and Hikari joined them.

"Looks like we have another member in our party," Cole said.

"You know, the more people we add to this party, the smaller our shares of the reward will be," Pal said.

"Tell me, friend, how did you come to be in such a precarious situation?" Hikari asked.

"I am but a traveler, a stranger to these lands. I was studying my spell book when I was ambushed by these foul creatures."

"I knew he was a sorcerer!" Cole exclaimed.

"Actually, I am a wizard. My magical abilities come from years of study and training. The white ribbon I've tied to my hand helps me conduct my spells. Some wizards prefer wands, but I am a ribbon man myself.

"A sorcerer's power is inherited. They were descendants of an ancient bloodline tracing back to the original masters of *mana*, the source of all magic. But unfortunately, they are extinct."

"What about magicians?" Cole asked.

The wizard spat. "Frauds. All of them."

"We can use a guy like you," Cole said.

"What is your name?" Hikari asked.

"I am Macario Nazaam. My father is Chief of the Maji Tribe. We are nomadic wizards who live on a peninsula west of the Idle Sea. I've been sent abroad in search of the meaning of life. If I solve this ancient riddle, I will have proved myself as a man and may return home."

"What if you can't solve it?" Cole asked.

"Then I must wander the world until I die," Macario said with an odd smile.

"You may journey with us, friend. I am Hikari Musha, Soldier of Light, Squire…"

"I'm Cole and this is my buddy, Pal."

"We already met."

Hikari and Pal headed back to the road.

"Come on, Macario," Cole said. "We don't want to get left behind."

"First, I must gather my spell books."

Macario waved his hand through the air and spoke arcane rhyme in a deep baritone.

"Charmed books, return to me
Find your place in the library."

The books scattered about the goblin camp flew into the air and sailed the shelves of Macario's backpack. "Shall we?" he asked.

They resumed their search for the gate to Elfwood. Cole filled Macario in on their mission. At the end of his long and embellished retelling of Princess Oriel's capture by a green dragon, Cole noticed Macario was not listening. In fact, Macario was not even there.

Cole retraced his steps and found the wizard a hundred yards behind them. Macario crouched, examining a large brown spider resting on a blade of grass. He picked it up and put it on his shoulder. When Cole saw the terrifying spider crawling on his new friend's shoulder, he drew Death's Edge.

"Macario, watch out! There's a spider on your shoulder," Cole shouted and raised his ax. "Don't worry. I think I can get it."

"Lower your weapon, my friend," Macario said. "I have invited this spider to join me on my quest as my familiar."

"Familiar?"

"All wizards are capable of making a magical bond with a single creature so we may tap into one another's energy pools."

"An animal-ally? I like that."

"But the creature must also choose me. Spiders are clever and make for exceptional familiars. Once the pact is made, only death may break it. A wizard must choose wisely, for one pact can be made in a lifetime."

Macario picked the spider up off of his shoulder. He held it in his open palm, and looked into the arachnid's beady black eyes. "So what do you think, my little friend? Shall we be life partners?"

The spider replied by biting Macario, who yelped and dropped it. Instinctively, he brought his palm to his mouth and sucked on the bite. "Spiders are also temperamental," he said.

Macario said,

"Itsy-bitsy spider halt,

Don't blame me, it's your own fault."

The spider froze. He picked the spider up and pulled off one of its legs. He set the spider on the ground, unfroze it, and it scuttled off. The severed leg, Macario dropped in a small jar.

"Don't worry, Macario," Cole said. "We have a whole journey for you to find your familiar."

Macario smiled, glanced down at his feet, and waved to the spider crawling back into the safety of the grass.

"Good day to you, spider. May you populate the world with many offspring." Macario whispered to Cole. "Their parting customs are different than ours, but they must be adhered to nonetheless."

Cole nodded and said, "Bye-bye, spider. Make babies."

Up ahead on the road, Pal and Hikari watched Cole and Macario wave goodbye to the spider.

"Wizards," Pal grumbled. "I don't trust them."

"I trust them as much as I trust rogues," Hikari said.

The rogue and paladin glared at each other. Trust would be a difficult gap to bridge, if it was even possible.

CHAPTER FIFTEEN

Fortune's Fool

The sun setting, a crescent moon appeared in the cloudy orange sky. Cole read a sign hanging above the door of a mysterious wagon on top of a hill:

FORTUNE TELLER

"Look, a gypsy!" he shouted. "Let's get our fortunes told!"

"I can tell your fortune," Macario said. "You're about to get ripped off."

A gorgeous zaftig gypsy stepped out from behind beads in the doorway of her wagon. Strands of pitch black hair fell out of her red shawl. A tiny black mole sat above her thin pursed lips. She hugged her round frame and leaned against the door, flaunting her curvy hips.

Pal smiled and said, "Don't be so negative, Macario."

"Evening gentlemen," the gypsy said with a voice as sultry as an August afternoon. "Can I interest any of you in a palm reading? Only costs a circ."

"Can I, Hikari? Can I? Can I? Can I?" Cole asked.

"It's your silver, Cole."

Macario's brow furrowed. Being a practitioner of the arcane arts, he detested those who pretended to wield magic. He stepped in front of Cole and told the gypsy, "The future has not been written, gypsy. You can do nothing but guess."

The gypsy played it cool. "You're a long way from home wizard, but don't fret," she said. "You'll make it back."

"Really?" Macario asked.

The gypsy closed her eyes, extended her hand as if reaching into the future. She chanted, "One shall scry and one will die. One betrays and one who slays. And one," she opened her eyes, "is not here."

"She's good," Cole said with excitement and tossed the gypsy a circ. She caught and bit it, took the coin from her mouth, and looked at the imprint left by her teeth. Satisfied, she said to Cole, "Step inside."

Dark, strange, and cozy, the gypsy's one room wagon served as living room, bedroom, kitchen, and office. The scent of strange perfumes filled Cole's nostrils and he coughed. The gypsy lit a stick of incense and a gray wisp of smoke slithered its way up to the low ceiling. Cole got caught in a web of beads as he entered the room.

"Nice place," he said.

Standing behind Cole, the gypsy said, "Sit."

Cole sat at a small circular table covered by a powder blue cloth. The gypsy was already sitting across from him.

"Your palm," she said.

Cole gave her his hand. The gypsy took it in hers and ran her red painted nails over Cole's lines and contours. It tickled, but Cole stifled a chuckle.

"You have a long marriage line. You will meet your true love, lose her, and reunite."

Cole drew his hand back, disappointed. "That's great and all, but what I want to know is, will I become a famous hero?"

"To know that, I need to consult the orb." With a flourish, the gypsy pulled a gossamer cloth off a globe that appeared in the center of the table. Cole was astounded.

The gypsy laid her hand on the dark globe, and milky smoke filled the orb as she called forth its power. She closed her eyes and the dark globe began to glow pink.

"You are a lover, not a fighter," the gypsy said in a detached voice.

"What?!"

"You will lead a life of adventure, but it will be full of heartache."

"Oh, come on."

The gypsy opened her eyes. They glowed the same pink as the globe. "Your fate is tied to the end of the world."

"That's more like it," Cole said rubbing his hands together.

The gypsy's eyes returned to their normal hazel color. "Could you please stop with the annoying comments?" she asked.

"Sorry."

The gypsy's eyes glowed pink again. "The world will face its end soon. A force of evil will bring Eld to the brink of destruction and you will be at the decisive battle."

"And then I save the world?" Cole asked.

"No," the gypsy said, her eyes hazel again. "You will fall in love with the one who does."

The globe darkened and Cole stared at the orb, waiting for more. "That's it?" he asked.

"Yes. For one more circ, I can tell you who you will fall in love with."

"You sure you got that right?" Cole asked and tapped the orb with his finger. "I mean, maybe this thing is broken."

The gypsy snatched the orb from Cole and said, "Do not question me. I do not decide your destiny, I am just the messenger."

Cole slammed his hands on the table and stood.

"Well, I want a second opinion!"

The rest of the party waited outside the wagon for Cole. Hikari studied his map of the Endless Forest. Macario chased a fox in circles proposing a magical partnership with the animal. Pal cleaned his dirty fingernails with the tip of his dagger.

Cole stormed out of the gypsy's wagon and passed the others.

"How did it go?" Pal asked.

"Let's get out of here," Cole said.

Macario allowed the fox scamper off into a hole and said, "I told you not to waste your money."

The gypsy stepped out of the wagon. She lit a wood pipe stuffed to the brim with tobacco, took a long satisfying drag, and watched Hikari, Cole, and Macario head off. Pal looked over his shoulder to catch one last glimpse of her and the gypsy stared at him. More accurately, she stared through him. She put her index finger and thumb to her lips and turned them like a key—the sign of the Locksmiths. Pal ran to catch up with the party.

CHAPTER SIXTEEN

Around the Campfire

Over the next few weeks, the party scoured the Endless Forest. Hikari made notes on the map, tracking the areas they had explored. The map was covered in Xs but they still had not found the gate to Elfwood. Each morning Pal slept until midday, needing his beauty sleep. Macario read his spell books, committing arcane rhymes to memory.

"Snake, wolf, frog, bat, and toad,
Give me the powers they behold"

Macario slithered, howled, hopped, flew, and croaked. Pal shot him dirty looks.

Hikari trained Cole in combat. It wasn't long before Cole noticed the flab on his belly shrunk and his leg muscles had grown and tightened. He was proud to punch a new hole into his old leather belt, to keep his trousers from falling.

During his search for a familiar, Macario made the acquaintance of a mink, a wild turkey, a ladybug, and a doe. None of them accepted his invitation. But Macario never seemed perturbed by the constant rejection. He explained to Cole, "If they do not want to be with me, I do not want to be with them."

Pal said, "That may go for bugs and birds, but when it comes to women, if you want her, keep charming her until you win her heart. It's a game of endurance."

Hikari offered no advice to Cole on the subject, although he disagreed with Pal. He resented the strange hold the rogue had over his pupil, fearing his influence would not end well.

Pal saw the enmity in the paladin's eyes, which only encouraged him to act with even worse manners than usual. He needled Hikari, criticizing his navigational skills. He also questioned little decisions like when to rest and where to sleep.

One day after many hours of traveling, Hikari found a suitable spot to camp. He unfurled his bedroll facing the direction of the sunset.

"We are nowhere near water and are down to our last water skin," the rogue said.

"We will have to tighten our rations," the paladin replied curtly.

Cole lowered a water skin from his lips. His cheeks swollen with the water he had been guzzling, he swallowed and stored the deerskin away.

"Shall we hunt?" Pal asked.

"You and Cole hunt tonight," Hikari grunted as he squatted to the ground and crossed his legs. He closed his eyes, trying to relax in the position. "I must pray and restore my powers."

"Riiight," Pal needled. "Are you sure you're not just trying to catch a nap old man?"

Hikari's eyes flashed open. "Old man?"

"Oh don't have a stroke. I was joking. Pray to your cloud god Puffy–"

Hikari sprung like a basilisk. "Never insult Rey!"

"Or what?" Pal stepped closer to Hikari, smiling as he goaded him. "Are fallen paladin excused from murder?"

Hikari didn't twitch. Neither did Pal. They battled each other with their eyes, glaring, waiting for the other to blink first. Macario kept silent but rolled his eyes in disapproval.

The awkward tension became palpable. Cole witnessed many fights at the orphanage, but all between children. Seeing two adults about to come to blows made him feel young and vulnerable. He needed to break the tension.

"Two goblins and an orc are in a carriage. Who's driving?"

They looked at him blankly.

"The constable."

Macario exploded with laughter. Cole chuckled, his eyes scanning Pal and Hikari's, hoping they were distracted from their feud. They were. Pal forced a large full bodied laugh and slapped Cole on the back.

"Funny stuff Cole. Come on. Let's go get us some dinner."

Cole and Pal spent the last few hours of daylight hunting. When they returned to camp with a rabbit for supper they found Macario reading a thick leather bound tome entitled, *The Art of Transmutation*. Hikari was bent over the fire stoking it with a twig and singing a hymn in his foreign tongue.

"That was a beautiful song," Cole said as he and Pal skinned the rabbit.

Hikari smiled. "It is an old song that my cleric used to sing to me."

"Can you translate the words?" Cole asked, his curiosity never satisfied.

"I praise Rey for his warmth and guidance in day and night, even when he is hidden."

"Worshipping something you can't even see. What a load of dung." Pal sneered and placed the skewered rabbit over the fire.

"Just because you can't see it, doesn't mean it's not there," Macario chimed in, not taking his eyes off his book.

Cole agreed with Macario but didn't say anything, as not to offend Pal.

"What do you believe Cole?" Hikari asked.

Cole frowned. "I'm not sure. Maybe someone isn't behind it all, but something. Something so powerful we will never be able truly to understand it. I don't know. I don't think about it that much."

Pal chimed in. "I believe in whatever helps you sleep at night."

Macario turned a page. "I believe there is a thirteenth plane of existence. There, an indescribable force that the first magic users named mana, influences all living and non-living things. It is something and yet it is nothing; a great mystery that cannot and should not be explained."

"Why wouldn't you want to explain it?" Cole asked.

"To put into words something you can only feel but not prove invites too many arguments. It is better to interpret the way the mystery makes *you* feel rather than to define what it is and try to force others to believe in your interpretation."

Cole contemplated what Macario said as he watched the rabbit's flesh roast over the flames.

After dinner, Macario entertained the group with prestidigitations. He changed Cole's hair color from blond to blue and back again. He made the water in their skins taste like elven nectar. He turned a bundle of kindling into a cutlery set. He soiled Hikari's pants. To cap off his performance he juggled globes of light.

Not to be shown up as the funny guy in the group, Cole told some of his favorite low-brow jokes. He told the one about the ogre with a hernia. And what the goblin wished for. He sang famous tavern songs about unmarried wenches and their fatherless children, which sent Macario and Pal into a side-splitting fit of laughter. Hikari did not find Cole's jokes amusing. Paladins do not enjoy potty humor.

Pal taught Cole and Macario to how to play dominoes and convinced them to gamble some of their forthcoming rewards. Hikari didn't want to play, so he studied the map of the Endless Forest, plotting the next day's course.

During one of the hands, Pal drained the last drop of water from his skin. He smacked his lips and said, "Ahhh." He held the skin high to distract the others and pocketed one of the magical knives. His distraction worked on Cole and Macario.

"I saw that," Hikari said, putting down the map.

"What?"

"Put the knife back."

Pal's face turned red hot. He pulled the knife out of his boot and threw it in the dirt, killing the jovial mood.

"It's fine. Of course, you can have the knife, Pal. It's just a twig. See?" Macario said and waved a hand over the knife twice, turning it back into a twig and back to a knife. "Please," he said and offered the magical twig knife to Pal, who stowed it in his boot.

Silence fell over the group. The tension between Pal and Hikari palpable, it was too much for Cole, who tried to lighten the mood.

"What do you get if you cross a cat with a lemon?" Cole asked.

No one asked and the punchline was never revealed. Pal glared at Hikari.

"What do you know about me, paladin?"

"I know your kind."

"My kind?"

"Thieves."

"I find it hard to believe you, a paladin, know anything about thieves."

"They are all the same."

"The one absolute truth about thieves is no two thieves are alike. They all have different limits, different goals, and different reasons for becoming who they are. You want to know the first thing I ever stole in my life? My freedom. I was born into slavery in some cursed country I don't even remember the name of. I was eight years old and already an expert temple builder. That's right. Who do you think builds your temples, paladin? Fairly paid laborers? Don't make me laugh.

"One day while I mixed clay, I overheard another slave say, 'No more. No more. No more.' He repeated it over and over, louder and louder, until all the slaves chanted, 'No more! No more! No more!' A whip cracked and the brave man's back split open. I remember looking at him, thinking how easily his flesh ripped.

"Madness erupted. Many died that day. But not me. I let the adults do the fighting and I stole off with some other kids. And I've been surviving ever since. How? Any way possible."

After a moment of silence, Cole said, "You don't have to worry anymore, Pal. From now on, you can always count on me to have your back."

"Same here," Macario said.

"How about you, Hikari?" Cole asked, urging the paladin to join in on the group love.

Hikari's lips squirmed. He set aside the map and knelt before Pal. "I admit I may have cast judgment too soon," he said. "Forgive me?"

Pal leaned back and refused eye contact. "Nothing to forgive," he said.

CHAPTER SEVENTEEN

The Gate

The following week, Pal and Hikari's breakthrough made for a more enjoyable journey. Each night around the campfire, Pal ran his dominoes game. Cole and Macario played while Hikari studied the map of the Endless Forest. They gambled with credit based on the reward money promised by King Langsley. Pal kept track of all monies won and lost in a tiny leather book.

One night after Pal cleaned out Macario and Cole again; Cole took Pal aside and asked him his secret to success.

"I cheat."

"But that's against the rules," Cole said.

Pal threw his arm around Cole. "I look at rules more like guidelines."

"Guidelines?"

"Trust me. Not everything is black and white. Sometimes you have to cheat to make sure you win. Because if you lose, think about who may win instead. The ends justify the means."

Cole pondered Pal's theory and concluded, "That's a pretty selfish point of view."

"In this world, you have to look out for yourself."

"No. That's what friends are for," Cole said. Miffed about getting swindled by his best friend, he shrugged off Pal's arm and rejoined the others at the campfire. To calm his nerves, he picked up Death's Edge and practiced his footwork.

Irritated by his guilt, Pal deliberately miscalculated some extra winnings for Cole. He deducted extra silver from Macario's share.

The next evening, after a long day of traveling, Hikari suggested they make camp.

"But we can't be far from the gate," Cole said. "I've got a good feeling about this."

"Go on if you like," Pal said. "But I need to rest."

"You guys always need to rest," Cole said.

"A hero must rest to rejuvenate strength," Hikari said.

"Fine," Cole said.

A warm clear evening, the party sat by the fire. Pal heard whispering in the bushes and said, "Excuse me a second."

"Where are you going?" Hikari asked.

"Taking a leak," Pal said. "Want to come?"

Hikari frowned and said, "Be quick and don't go too far."

"Yes, mother," Pal said and walked off.

Hikari shook his head. At his side, curled in a ball, Cole slept.

Pal made his way through the forest until the camp was out of sight. He found a tree, unbuttoned his breeches, and relieved himself. When he was done, he noticed an arrow wedged in the base of the tree. Another note was written on tiny rolled up parchment. Pal removed the scroll from the arrow and read:

First a paladin, now a wizard. My trust in you decreases by the day.

The scroll dissolved into dust and a breeze carried Sarik's message away.

Hikari's voice startled Pal. "I do not know what you are up to, but if you put me or the others in danger, I will not hesitate to strike you down."

Pal's shoulders lowered. His voice regained its cool, level pitch. "I'll keep that in mind," he said and brushed past Hikari.

"Pal," the paladin said.

"What?"

Hikari nodded to Pal's breeches. "Button up. I would not want you to catch a cold."

Pal buttoned his trousers and headed back to the camp. When Hikari was alone, he saw the arrow lodged in the tree and could swear he heard faint whispers on the wind.

Deep into the night, after the moon had reached its peak and stars glittered in the sky, the entire party was fast asleep. Besides the crickets and creaking of tree branches, it was quiet in the camp.

A distant clip clop, clip clop, clip clop of hooves trotted toward the sleeping men. Tiny white lights danced around the camp, and when one of the luminescent motes fell on Cole's nose, he woke. It was like a snowflake had fallen and melted against his skin. Not unpleasant, but unexpected and startling. He grabbed Death's Edge, ready to fight. The magical flurries swirled around him and he relaxed. A sense of wonder took hold of him, the way a child witnessing snow for the first time watches in silent awe.

Cole whispered, "Hikari. Pal. Macario. You guys see this?"

None of them woke, not even when a shining unicorn galloped into the camp. The magnificent beast resembled a horse, but larger and full of vitality. Her coat was snow white, as was its long curled mane. A ribbed horn stretched from her forehead, sparkling with magic.

Cole lowered his ax. The weapon felt wrong in his hands so close to the unicorn. He'd never seen anything more enchanting in his life. He had to touch her. He swung Death's Edge over his shoulder. Slowly, Cole approached the unicorn, trying his best not to scare her away. Her dark gray eyes were mirrors; he could not read the unicorn's temperament. All he saw was his own astonished expression growing larger with each step.

Only a few feet away, he extended his hand, raising it cautiously. The unicorn stood its ground, blinking calmly. Cole's fingers were inches from her neck when she whinnied and galloped off into the woods. Cole raced after her.

He followed the unicorn to an ancient gate standing alone in the middle of the forest. The word *Elfwood* was written in iron above the arch.

"The gate to Elfwood," he said to himself and turned to the unicorn. "Thank you."

The unicorn nodded her head as if she understood him, trotted up to Cole, forcing him a few steps back. She snorted and scraped her hooves against the earth, beckoning him to pet her. He ran his fingers through her thick snowy mane and up the horn. Cole smiled as a warm and comforting sensation emanating from the horn filled his spirit. Thus far, it was the single greatest moment of his life.

Thhhp! Cole looked down and found an arrow planted in his gut. The unicorn neighed a warning before two goblins jumped down from the trees above and tackled it. Cole dropped to his knees, crippled with pain. His muscles contracted around the arrow. He helplessly watched the goblins wrestle with the unicorn. Heavy footsteps shook the ground behind him. He rolled his head back over his shoulder and looked up into the face of a hobgoblin.

Hobgoblins, members of the goblin family, are twice as big as a man and meaner than a bad case of diarrhea. Not particularly intelligent, but dangerous, the slobbery monsters rely on strength and fear to take down their prey. Which Cole was about to find out.

The hobgoblin lowered its broad droopy bulldog face to Cole. Necklaces of drool hung from the corners of the hobgoblin's thick lips. It opened its mouth and panted with excitement. *Dinner!* it thought.

Cole was revolted by the hairy giant goblin. Its breath smelled of death and its armpits smelled worse. The stench was so putrid, Cole's eyes began to water.

The hobgoblin raised a club, a massive tree branch, and slugged Cole. He landed on his back ten feet away. His ears rang, and momentarily, he lost sight in his left eye.

When vision returned, Cole saw the goblins riding wildly on the unicorn's back. They drew short swords and stabbed her snow white flank. Silver blood leaked from the wounds.

"No!" Cole bellowed, mustered his strength, and stumbled to the unicorn's aid.

Another arrow flew through the air and pierced Cole's calf. He dropped again. A third goblin equipped with a crossbow stepped out from behind a tree and pumped its fist in triumph.

The hobgoblin stomped over to Cole and raised its club. Human pudding was on the menu tonight. A tongue the size of a hand wet the monster's lips. The hobgoblin brought the club down. Grass and dirt sprayed into the air. Cole rolled away, barely escaping the club's wrath. The hobgoblin growled in frustration.

Cole unslung Death's Edge and took an offensive stance. He raised the ax and brought it down on the hobgoblin, lodging it into the monster's side. The hobgoblin cried in pain and backhanded Cole. It took the ax from its side and licked the black blood from the blade and then snapped the weapon in two. It was like the wind was knocked out of Cole. His most precious possession destroyed, he shouted like a madman and jumped onto the hobgoblin's back. He grasped handfuls of its fiery orange hair and climbed up the fiend's back to strangle it.

Behind the trees, the goblin archer reloaded its crossbow and aimed at Cole. The hobgoblin roared and spun just as the arrow intended for Cole pierced its chest. The hobgoblin howled again, grabbed Cole by his collar, and threw him aside. The goblin archer shrieked in distress. *Whoops!* The hobgoblin rushed over to the goblin archer, grabbed it by the torso and bit its head off.

The unicorn ran in circles around Cole and the hobgoblin, braying and kicking, a hellish merry-go-round, desperate to be rid of the attacking goblins. She galloped alongside a cluster of trees and squashed one of the goblins against them. The other goblin maintained its balance and plunged a sword into the unicorn's shoulder. The unicorn's whinny was thick with blood and ended abruptly when she tumbled. The goblin drew its silver-blood drenched sword from the unicorn and delivered a coup de grace.

Cole watched from the grass in horror. It was too late to save her, but he would not let the unicorn die unavenged. Shouting his ferocious battle cry, he tackled the goblin. He straddled the monster and pummeled its face with his fists.

The hobgoblin chewed on the head of the goblin archer. A dreadful smacking of flesh against teeth, the goblin was bubblegum to the hobgoblin. When the skull had been cleaned of all its meat, the hobgoblin spat it out like a seed. It noticed Cole—*dessert!*

Cole mashed the unicorn murderer's brains into the grass. His knuckles were raw and sore and drenched in black blood, but he still hungered for vengeance.

A shadow loomed over him. By instinct, he tumbled away, barely dodging the hobgoblin's massive club a second time. The club shattered into a hundred splinters. The livid hobgoblin foamed at the mouth and threw the shaft aside to face off against Cole.

"Okay, ugly," Cole said. "Time to meet your maker!"

He propelled himself at the hobgoblin but was easily thrashed unconscious. Growling delightfully the monster picked Cole up by his hair. Savoring his well-earned meal, the hobgoblin opened its mouth and licked Cole with its massive purple tongue. Cole's eyes flashed open.

"Chew on this!" he shouted and drove a splinter he'd secreted from the club into the hobgoblin's eye. The hobgoblin howled, threw Cole into a tree beside the unicorn, and ran away crying.

His life hung by a thread, but Cole used the last ounce of energy to crawl over to the unicorn. Her vacant eyes were open and as reflective as before. Cole saw his face purpling with bruises. His teeth were shattered and his skin hung from his skull.

"I'm sorry. I tried."

Cole pet her gently. The unicorn's horn glowed and magically separated from her head. The spiraling grooved horn fell into his hand. He felt healing magic course through his body from the horn. In the blink of a shooting star the pain ravaging his body evaporated. Cole was dumbfounded. He stood with ease and ran his fingers over his face. His bruises disappeared. His wounds sealed. He checked with his tongue and found his teeth were restored.

Cole gazed reverently at the horn in his grasp. He was saved. How? He could not fathom. But why? He knew it was the horn.

A garrote thrown over his neck interrupted his train of thought. A camouflaged elven ranger tightened the grip until Cole blacked out.

CHAPTER EIGHTEEN

Elfwood

The fleeing hobgoblin's heavy footsteps woke Hikari. He leaped to his feet, and drew the Sun Sword. The camp became so bright, it was as if the sun had risen. Pal and Macario woke.

"What's wrong?" Macario asked, rubbing his sleepy eyes.

"I think we're sharing a nightmare," Pal said.

The hobgoblin roared as it approached, hoping to scare away the humans. It had had its fill of fighting for the night. Hikari sidestepped the monster and made a single cut along the hobgoblin's middle. Its legs kept running forward but the upper body fell.

Pal stood. "We need to start taking shifts on lookout."

Macario pinched his nose. "Agreed. If we didn't see the hobgoblin, we would have smelled him."

"Where's Cole?" Hikari asked.

The party ran through the forest, Hikari's sword lighting their way. Pal followed the kicked up grass and impressions of hooves and large boots in the disturbed mud.

"Cole's tracks lead this way," Pal said. "That's odd. It looks like he chased a wild horse."

Hikari huffed. "When we find that boy, we're going to have a long talk about chasing wild animals."

"I hope the horse is friendly. I've never known a wizard with a horse familiar and it would be a boon on this adventure."

"Not now, Macario," Pal shouted.

The party picked up their pace, and within minutes, arrived at the gate.

"The gate to Elfwood," Macario said astonished.

Hikari took in the carnage. A sword protruded from the neck of a dead white horse. The bodies of dead goblins were strewn about the gruesome scene.

"Goblins," Hikari growled.

"But no Cole," Macario said.

Hikari gasped. His eye caught Death's Edge, split in two. He kneeled and wept. Macario stood behind Hikari. He wanted to comfort him, but didn't know what to say.

"He's not dead," Pal cried. "Look!" He followed tracks leading to the closed iron gate. "He was captured and dragged through here." Pal circled to the other side of the gate, frowned, and concluded, "It doesn't make sense. The tracks don't continue on the other side."

"Of course they don't," Macario said as if it was obvious. "The universe is like a book and each page is a plane of existence. These gates are portals to the worlds behind our world. The tracks must continue in Elfwood. But who would kidnap Cole?"

"Elves," Hikari said with bitterness. "King Langsley was right to warn us. They have no love for humans. They have given up on our race." Hikari pulled on the rusted iron bars. "It won't budge."

"Stand back," Pal said, "I can pick the lock." He reached into an inner breast pocket and retrieved a worn roll of dark fabric. He unlaced its red string and unrolled the bundle. It housed small picks, hooks, grips, and lifts. Pal glanced again at the gate and picked his first tool. His nimble fingers went to work. In a matter of moments, a satisfying click unlocked the gate.

"Ta-da!" Pal said. "You can all thank me later."

Hikari, too preoccupied with worry, didn't mind Pal's showmanship. He was just thankful they were able to follow Cole into the Elfwood.

Pal swung the gate open, which emitted a shrill creak. From this side of the gate, nothing changed, but once they looked through...

The night turned to day. They saw a perfect mirror image of the Endless Forest, but with one drastic difference: the land of Elfwood was alive. The trees and grass breathed. Colors were vibrant. Birds sang joyful riffs and swam in the air.

Hikari sheathed his sword and marched through the gate, leaving the night behind him. Macario followed, skipping with excitement. He called for Pal to come on before heading into the mysterious lands of Elfwood.

The rogue, followed but paused when he crossed the threshold and looked back. On the other side of the gate, it was night. Pal drew a dagger and wedged it between the ground and the gate. It would stay open for the Locksmiths to follow them. Satisfied with his improvised doorstop, Pal ran and caught up with the others.

CHAPTER NINETEEN

Elven Hospitality

The first elves built Elfwick, a fortress carved into a sequoia tree stretching a mile high. With great care and purpose, they wasted not a single resource in its construction. Hollowed roots served as barracks for the queen's rangers and the king's soldiers. Its trunk accommodated training facilities, armories, and bed chambers for the civilian population. Great branches canopied by vast golden needle leaves housed giant luxury nests. These were occupied by the highest ranking elves. A village of tents populated by centaurs, gnomes, satyrs, leprechauns, and nymphs—all races of the Fair Folk—flourished around the base of the tree. They were welcome to live under the protection of the elves, but none were permitted to live within the walls of Elfwick, a special honor reserved only for elven pure-bloods.

The main entrance to the fortress was an arched door, carved between two of the sequoia's biggest roots. Etched into the door were traditional elven designs of wildlife and flora. The door split and opened for the returning elven rangers and their prisoner.

The rangers dragged Cole into the courtroom, an immense cavity in the tree. The smooth sapwood walls stretched to the ceiling of exposed heartwood. The room smelled like sweet vanilla. Doves perched on open windows gazed down at the disheveled prisoner. It had been a century or longer since a human had set foot in the court. They cooed and fluttered away, having no desire to witness what was sure to be a swift trial.

Cole walked between rows of elves sitting cross-legged. They hummed a folk song in harmony while knitting camouflaged cloaks for the queen's rangers. The needlesticks ticktocking to the tempo of their song stopped as Cole passed. Enthralled by the resplendence of the elves, for a moment, Cole forgot his predicament. They were beautiful. Smooth, dark skin the color of tree bark. Long pointed ears. Wise azure eyes. They wore billowing earth-toned cloaks and tightly knitted fabric belts. The straps of their sandals wove up their legs in intricate designs. All the elves possessed regal appearance, but their demeanor was unpleasant and judgmental. None more so than the elven queen.

Although she was the most powerful elf in the kingdom, she dressed modestly. The elven queen wore a blooming chaplet and a simple chocolate gown. It was conservatively cut and hung perfectly on her lithe frame. Poised and elegant, she watched the team of elven rangers push a large blond human to his knees at the foot of her pinecone throne.

She eyed Cole, then turned to the ranger captain. "Why do you bring this *human* before me, Domina?" Her emphasis on the word *human* made Cole feel objectified and outcast. He wished Hikari was with him. He would know what to do.

The ranger captain stepped forward and pulled back her camouflaged hood. She revealed a youthful face as fierce as it was fair. She looked striking similarity to the queen. Her black hair was drawn back and tied in tight elven military regulation braids. Her face was round and her cheekbones high. Cole would have guessed she was the same age as him, but she was actually seven hundred years older.

Although Cole did not know it at the time, the imposing ranger named Domina was captain of the elven infantry. Her two pegasus feathers worn like an X at the back of her head signified her high status. Her accompanying rangers were mere privates, and wore full headdresses. (Concerning elves, less is more. So you may forgive Cole for mistaking the woman with two feathers being of lesser rank than her inferiors. Had he seen a general who wore a single feather upright at twelve o'clock, he would have thought him irrelevant. An easy way to distinguish elven military ranking: the more feathers the lower the rank. Soldiers wear their feathers between one and eleven o'clock; infantry wore feathers upright, artillery wore feathers downright, and cavalry wore feathers with the wind.)

"We caught him slaying a unicorn, Mother."

Domina held out the horn. The entire court gasped. An elven minister fainted. Guards strangled their halberds, wishing they were Cole's neck. The elven queen's rage visible, her eyes widened and her lips quivered with fury.

Cole began to defend himself. "I tried to save the..."

"Silence, *human*!" The elven queen exclaimed, stood, and raised an accusing finger at Cole. "Your race is despicable. You squander Mud'hir Erta's gifts and lay waste to her lands. That is why your kind was banished from Elfwood. We elves have tolerated your shortcomings for too long. But the murder of a unicorn is unforgivable. Throw him in the dungeons with the warlock."

Shocked murmuring buzzed around the court. Cole's heart hammered in his chest and his throat went dry. Whoever this warlock was, based on the court's reaction, he had no desire to find out.

Domina could not believe the command either, and for a moment, forgot her place. "But mother!"

"Do as I say, Domina."

Domina bowed her head and said, "Yes mother."

She whistled, and two of her rangers grabbed Cole's arms. They dragged him kicking and protesting his innocence out of the courtroom. The elven queen raised her chin, thinking his punishment just. The human would be subjected to the nefarious company of the warlock before he would die. Tomorrow.

Underground, in the deepest roots of Elfwick, were the dungeons. Hollowed poles of wood and palm leaf fans ventilated the prison. However, the limited oxygen made the prisoners and guards a little light headed and loopy.

Domina and her two rangers escorted him down a long hallway of cells at the bottom of the dungeons. Cole glanced into the small barred cells on either side of him. The prisoners paid him no notice. They had long ago resigned themselves to their fate and did not give a lick about a new prisoner.

At the end of the hallway, behind a thick steel door, was the only enclosed cell and the only cell made of metal. Bolts, locks, and chains protected anyone from entering or leaving. A knee-high slot for food was also locked shut. Beside the door was the warden's station. There was a small wooden desk with a ledger of prisoners and a bottle of elven nectar. The warden and his deputy were not supposed to be drinking on duty.

The warden's plump gut hung over his belt. His cropped hair was white, and five earrings were pierced in each of his pointed ears. The deputy was tall and youthful, despite only being four hundred years old. The warden may have been nearing a thousand, though. At a certain point in every elf's life, they stop counting.

As Domina approached, the warden hid the bottle of mead and opened the ledger to look busy. "What brings you down to our level, your highness?" the warden asked.

"I brought the warlock a new cell mate."

The deputy laughed in disbelief.

"But your highness..." the warden began.

"My orders come directly from the queen," Domina interrupted.

The warden and his deputy looked at each other and warily at the steel door. Once more they looked at Domina, who confirmed her order with an impatient glare. The warden unlocked the door and opened it, and the deputy dipped a quill in ink and offered it and the ledger to Cole.

"S-s-sign here," the deputy stuttered.

The rangers loosened their grip. Cole took the quill and signed the ledger. Accounted for, he was shoved into the dark cell. The door slammed shut behind him.

Cole's stomach somersaulted and his knees gave way. He collapsed onto the cold floor as the room spun around him. He dry heaved until his lungs ached. It was a tortuous minute until the world seemed to regain its equilibrium.

Cole heard muffled, low-pitched words spoken outside. He crawled to the door to press an ear against the cold steel, but couldn't make out a single word. The elves outside spoke at a snail's pace, and listening made Cole dizzy.

The knee-high slot slid open and a tray of stale elven bread and a wooden mug filled with water was served. Cole kicked them aside.

"I would eat if I were you," a melodious voice came from the darkness.

Cole spun around. At first glance, the room was empty. There was only a cot, a squat toilet, and a crooked mirror hanging on the wall behind a set of iron bars.

"Who said that?"

"Just a weary old man," the voice replied.

Cole approached the mirror and realized it was not a mirror after all. It cast no reflection. In its frame was another cell, where an old man with pale wrinkled skin and two viridescent eyes sat on a cot. His receding gray hair was combed into a ducktail with two horned tufts curling at the sides. His eyebrows were sharp and expressive. A dark cloak wrapped around him made him look small and frail. He repeatedly straightened his cloak and compulsively smoothed its fabric. For all the fuss the elves made, Cole was not impressed.

"Are you the warlock?" Cole asked.

"My name is Il i'Tir. And you are?"

"Cole. What are you in here for?"

"I killed the elven king," the warlock answered matter-of-factly.

Now Cole was impressed. And scared. He tried to casually back away.

"Don't be afraid. The elven king attacked me and my daughter in battle. It was self-defense," the warlock said and drew his cloak tighter around his torso. "The elves, however, have a different point of view."

Cole nodded his head in agreement.

"What did you do?" the warlock inquired.

"Nothing."

"Oh, come on. The elves would not throw you in with big bad me unless you did something terrible."

Cole sighed and stared at his feet. "They accuse me of killing a unicorn." It was painful to speak the words. If there was ever a being in this world Cole would never harm, it was a unicorn.

The warlock raised his eyebrows. "Did you?"

"No!" Cole kicked the steel door of the cell. "Those good for nothing, rotten elves!" he exclaimed. "I tried to save the unicorn from a hobgoblin attack. They didn't even give me a chance to explain."

"So, you're a hero?"

"That's right," Cole said as he picked up the bread. He took a bite and gagged. Full of nutrients, it was hearty but dry. He drank his cup of water at once. He addressed his cellmate. "They're not going to put me in a mirror, are they?"

"I should hope not. It's extremely uncomfortable in here."

Cole slumped down against the steel door. "I wish they'd kill me and get it over with."

Il i'Tir stood and approached the glass of his mirror prison to get a better look at Cole. His breath fogged the glass. "Oh, they'll kill you. Eventually. But first, they're going to bore you to death. So you might as well relax. You're going to be in here for a long time."

Cole slammed his elbow against the steel door, making it ring. He ignored the pain shooting up his arm said, "If I ever get out of here, I'm gonna cut that stupid elven queen's head off."

Il i'Tir smiled. "I have the feeling you and I are going to become good friends."

CHAPTER TWENTY

The Prisoner

Cole spent almost four years locked in the cell with the warlock. After the first twenty-nine days and no rescue, Cole's spirit broke. He resigned himself to a lifetime in captivity with the warlock. Every morning, he woke and scratched another tally into the wall with his sharpened belt prong. Each night he cried himself to sleep.

The warlock imprisoned in the magic mirror on the wall kept to himself. Most days, Il i'Tir dozed coiled on his cot, a sleeping serpent. Other times, he sat, silently gazing at his cell walls. *Thinking. Always thinking. Of what?* Cole wondered, but never dared ask.

For some men, prison changes them. For others, it deepens what was already there. The latter was the case for Cole. Yes, they broke his spirit, and hopes of being rescued. But he was never reborn into the submissive prisoner the elves hoped he would become. He clung to his childhood dream of becoming a hero more than ever. His warped sense of self-importance flourished. His memories of victory in battle became exaggerated to a point beyond belief. All the small accomplishments done in distant days became great deeds in his mind. He saw himself as a martyr.

It was on day thirty, out of sheer boredom, Cole began to exercise. Stretching and pushing his muscles to their limit was his only therapeutic release. He followed a strict regime—a diluted version of Hikari's morning training routine—but it gave him purpose. Routine saves a man. It keeps him straight on the narrow path of sanity. Each morning, Cole would wake and do jumping jacks, push-ups, sit-ups, dips, squats, crunches, and run in thousands of circles around his cell. He exercised under the ever-present gaze of the warlock.

Outside Cole's cell, the warden flipped over a minute glass. The sand streamed down into the empty bulb below and he ordered his deputy to feed the prisoner again. Each minute outside of Cole's cell equaled one day inside. The enchantment was cast by the elves greatest allies and cousins, the sylvans. Occasionally referred to as high elves, they lived in the mountains. While the elves were one with the forests, the sylvans had an affinity for precious metals and the mysteries of magic. During the constructions of Elfwick's dungeons, the sylvans built the magic prison Cole occupied. They also crafted the magic mirror that trapped the warlock.

It was the one thousand and one hundred-fortieth time the warden had flipped the minute glass over; only the nineteenth hour of Cole's imprisonment. An excruciatingly boring job, the warden ordered his deputy to keep track of time while he took a nap. Only five more hours to go until Cole would be executed and the warden could go back to business as usual.

A new tray of elven bread and a wooden cup of water slid into the room. Cole snatched up the small loaf and gobbled it down, guzzled the water, and ate his meal and was full. The tray was pulled out of the room and the knee-high door slid shut. It would not open again for another day.

Another day gone, Cole thought. He scratched a new tally into the wall, and began his daily exercise routine. He had become unrecognizable to the young man who left Flounder all those years ago. His blond hair had grown down past his shoulders. An untrimmed beard hung from his gaunt face. There was no longer an ounce of fat on his body. His muscles were tight and lean, but he looked weak because his large frame craved nutrients absent from his prison diet. When Cole finished exercising, he was hungry again. It had been the cycle for the past three years: eat, exercise, starve, rest, and wait for the next day.

Cole lay on his cot and stared at the walls of his cell trying to ignore his growling stomach. Two walls covered with tallies, Cole started on the third. It was impressive, all the tallies, over a thousand tiny white marks dug into the walls. His belt prong had whittled away over the years and was no bigger than a tooth now. What would he do when it was gone? How would he calculate time? He shivered and decided not to think about such depressing thoughts. He needed to cheer himself up. He needed a story.

"Il?"

The warlock grunted from his cot.

"Did I ever tell you the time I defeated the bullies at the orphanage?"

"Yes."

"Oh, right. Of course. How about when..."

"Cole, some of us in here are not as lucky as you."

Cole propped himself up on his elbow, turned to the mirror, and asked, "How do you figure?"

"I have not eaten since I was captured. I have to conserve my energy to stay alive."

"Oh, right. Of course. How do you stay alive without food?"

"I go into hibernation."

"Oh, right. Of course. How do you..."

"Cole?"

"Yes?"

"Shut up."

Cole remained silent for the rest of the day. Time crawled like morning fog. He spent his day reliving memories he'd rather be sharing with his cellmate. He was so lost in his thoughts; Cole didn't realize he spoke aloud. It wasn't until he stopped reciting a lengthy tale about a tax collector Cole proved to be corrupt, Il i'Tir spoke.

"Why are you so obsessed with being a hero?"

Glad to be ripped from his solitary reverie, Cole said, "Because I want to be remembered after I die."

"You don't have to be a hero to be remembered. Don't you think your family will remember you regardless of your accomplishments?"

Cole said, "I don't have a family."

Irritated by Cole's stupidity, the warlock clicked his tongue and said, "Everyone has a family."

"Not me. I'm an orphan. If I had parents, they didn't want me."

The shadow of a grin creeping up the warlock's mouth, he nodded, feigning empathy, and said, "Ah. I see. So, this dream of yours is to prove your parents wrong?"

"No."

"To humiliate them and make them feel guilty for abandoning you?"

Cole frowned. "No."

The warlock stood. He menacingly approached the glass wall of his prison. "You lay on your cot, bragging of such small accomplishments, but all you desire is for someone to tell you you're not worthless."

"No!" Cole shouted, and trembled with a familiar mixture of rage and embarrassment. The war drums beat faintly in his ears.

"I find it pathetic," Il i'Tir said. "Not your desire for achievement, but your shameless self-promotion of incidental deeds. You proclaim yourself a hero, but why? What, in the great scheme of things, have you achieved? Who is happier, knowing Cole is out there somewhere, defending the world from embezzling lawmen?"

"Shut up!"

Cole slammed his fists against the bars protecting the mirror. His skinny, starved hands, slipped through and hit the glass. A spider web of cracks appeared, silencing the warlock.

Cole's heart thundered in his chest; tears of rage welled up in the corners of his eyes. He pulled his hands out from between the bars and collapsed onto his cot. He spent the remaining hours of the day weeping. The knee-high slot in the steel door slid open and a tray of elven bread and cup of water appeared.

He didn't bother to tally the new day on his cell wall.

CHAPTER TWENTY-ONE

Ambush

Hikari, Pal, and Macario spent more than half a day fruitlessly searching Elfwood for Cole. As the paladin, rogue, and wizard looked for their missing friend, the landscape shifted and circled, and always led them back to the gate where they began.

Macario found the infinite possibilities of travel fascinating and exclaimed, "Wondrous!" and "Inconceivable!" and "Well I never..." at all the oddities.

The confusion began to drive Pal crazy. "Anyone else see this?" he asked, rubbing his eyes, exasperated.

"Yes," Macario said, squealing with delight. "Isn't it pretty? I've read about such occurrences in Elfwood, but to see them with my own eyes is a wonder to behold."

"What do you know of Elfwood, Macario?" Hikari asked.

Macario held out his hand, and said,

"Okay books, you know the drill,

The Gatewalkers Guide, if you will."

A maroon hardcover book entitled *The 13 Planes: A Guide for Gatewalkers* flew off of a shelf of his backpack-library and into his grasp. Macario skimmed the book. He found a chapter on Elfwood, and read the relevant paragraph aloud. "Elfwood exists on a parallel plane that defies the laws of reality. Time is fluid here. It has no standard and chooses its length as it pleases. Gatewalkers may find these inconsistencies dizzying. Therefore, it is suggested that you travel between planes on an empty stomach."

"You speak as if time has a choice here," Pal said.

Macario smiled. "It does. For all we know, we could have been searching for centuries or seconds. Or both." He snapped the book shut and sent it back to its place in his portable library wedged between *Interplanar Alignment,* a history book, and a lighter read, *Mana Maniacs! The Most Villainous Wizards of All Time.*

For hours or days or minutes or years, it was impossible for Hikari to keep track, they searched, but found no trace of Cole. Day turned to night, and in the blink of an eye, it was day again.

The longer they searched, the deeper the lines on Hikari's forehead grew. The brazen but endearing boy had become closer to him than just a pupil. Cole had become a brother. He needed guidance. He needed training. He needed Hikari and Hikari needed Cole. Many years ago, Hikari vowed he would never fail a brother again. He was determined to search until the boy was found or die trying.

Time dragged on and success seemed less and less likely. Hikari fell deeper into despair. He muttered desperate prayers, imploring his lord Rey to illuminate the right path, lest he dishonor himself again.

"I don't like this place," Pal said from the rear of the group, contending with an acidic burp stuck in his throat. "I feel sick."

"A common side effect," Macario said. "If we were to base time according to when we began our search, we have been walking for no longer than fifteen hours and no less than fourteen."

"Pretty exact," Hikari said.

"I've been counting my footsteps since we began our interplanar travel," Macario said. "And if my calculations are correct, I would estimate I take approximately one step per second which equals..."

"Quiet," Hikari said, brandishing the Sun Sword.

The party waited in illuminated silence. The only sound was the hum of Hikari's iridescent sword.

"False alarm." Hikari lowered his weapon, although his intuition did not often fail him.

Forgetting their feud for a second, Pal rested a hand on Hikari's shoulder and said, "We're all tired. We should rest."

"No," Hikari said. "We must journey forth. The longer Cole is gone, the less likely we will be able to find him."

"Wait," Pal said. "I do hear something."

Macario listened. "It sounds like a swarm of bees."

Hikari drew his katana, Pal his daggers, and Macario put up his dukes. They took cautious steps forward, ready for anything.

A storm of arrows rained down on them. With acrobatic grace, Pal tumbled to safety. Hikari spun the Sun Sword like a propeller. He severed the arrows spiraling towards them. Macario turned and five arrows planted themselves in the books of his backpack library. He glanced up into the trees and saw camouflaged figures reloading their longbows.

"Elves!" he exclaimed.

Another volley of arrows rained on them. Hikari fried the advancing arrows with a holy beam of sunlight from his sword. Pal grabbed Macario and shoved him behind a tree for protection.

"You saved me again," Macario said. "At this rate, I will be indebted to you forever."

Pal shuddered at the thought. "What do we do now?"

"They must think we mean them harm," Macario said. "Whatever you do, do not fight back."

An arrow landed right between Pal's legs.

Domina lowered her bow and smiled. She threw up a clenched fist and her rangers lowered their loaded bows. She jumped down from her perch with calculated grace. Her troops of camouflaged rangers followed suit, landing behind her. She drew her short sword. Carved from ironwood and shaved deadly thin, she pushed a button on the hilt, and unlocked a second sword. It fell into her free hand. The other rangers followed suit.

"Half to the paladin and half to the wizard. The rogue is mine," she said. The rangers raised their swords above their heads like an X and stormed their prey.

Hikari defended himself against ten elven rangers in an uneven fight of twenty swords against one. Channeling all his frustration, he funneled his god's divine favor into his holy weapon. He deftly parried and sundered their attacks with the blazing Sun Sword.

Untrained in combat, Macario needed time to think of an appropriate spell. Wizards are only as powerful as they are creative. In the heat of battle, most wizards freeze up and pay with their lives. This was not a price Macario was willing to pay.

Macario did his best to follow his own advice and did not attack the elves. After several failed attempts at diplomacy, he unfurled a scroll and read the arcane rhyme aloud.

"Charm these leaves and make them rise

I need a place for me to hide."

A ten-foot high curtain of leaves appeared. He hid from the unending volley of arrows.

"Contrary to how this appears, we mean you no harm," Macario shouted over the whizzing arrows.

The elven rangers had no pity for Macario's friendly pleas. He was a human and it was forbidden for humans to enter the Elfwood. They continued to nock and fire arrows. Three rangers ran to flank the wizard.

Center stage in the fight, Pal and Domina engaged in a deadly dance of two-handed sword-play. Domina twirled her swords, a wooden zephyr, and they clacked off Pal's perfectly timed parries.

"You fight well...for a human."

"You fight well...for a girl."

Big mistake.

Domina squinted her eyes and snarled. She had been holding back to test the swarthy human's skills. With a feral roar she advanced, and within seconds had the upper hand. Using her swords like shears, Domina overwhelmed Pal. She scissored the daggers out of his hands. Before Pal could draw another pair, he had two elven blades at his throat.

"I could cut off your head with one stroke," she sneered.

Pal called for help, never taking his eyes off the threatening elven beauty. "Macario! Now would be the time to make good on your promise."

Macario paced back and forth, skimming his book *Everything You Need To Know About Elves* for a diplomatic solution. An arrow pierced the green hardcover binding of his book. Macario looked up and saw the elven rangers at his flank. Each drew one sword and pushed a release button, which made two. Macario gulped and did the first thing that came to mind. He ran.

Out of his periphery, Hikari saw Pal and the two blades at his throat. With a mighty swing of his holy katana, he broke free from his engagement. A wave of heat knocked his assailants prone. Fury glinting in his eyes, he charged at Domina with the Sun Sword above his head. A step away, Domina turned and held the tip of her left sword to his throat.

"Please," she said. "Take another step forward."

Conceding defeat, Hikari lowered his weapon. He kept his eyes fixed on Domina as the elven rangers disarmed him and bound his hands behind his back.

"Domina. The wizard is gone," one of the rangers reported.

"Forget him," she said. "Three humans in one day is fine with me."

"Cole? You have Cole?" Pal asked.

"Gag them," Domina said.

Before Hikari or Pal could respond, the rangers silenced them. Pal glared at Domina, his mouth full of dry cloth. She smiled victoriously at him and mobilized her troops of rangers.

Pal smirked. *This isn't over yet, elf*, he thought and dug his nails into his palm. Small drops of his blood left a trail for the Locksmiths to follow.

CHAPTER TWENTY-TWO

The Tale of Il i'Tir

Cole did not speak with Il i'Tir for days after their rift. He gave the warlock the silent treatment for a week and he stopped tallying his days. In fact, he stopped eating as well. Six loaves of bread stacked up near the door. Cole drank his daily cup of water, but that was all he put into his body. The rest of his days he spent lying with his back to the barred magic mirror.

When his stomach began to growl, the warlock begged him to eat. Cole ignored him and fasted. All he wanted was to die. At least he thought so until the warlock said, "I apologize."

Cole rolled over. His unfocused eyes flickered in the dim cell.

The warlock admitted, "I spoke out of frustration. For decades, I have been the sole occupant of this cell...and one-day...you show up.

"At first I thought the elven queen sent you as my punishment. Pair the wretched warlock Il i'Tir with an imbecile to torment him further." Cole frowned. Il i'Tir raised a pleading hand and went on, "But now I know the opposite to be true. *I* am *your* punishment. You have been sentenced to death, but my sentence is to rot.

"While you will at least taste the sweet air once more on your judgment day, I will never have a reprieve from my cell. I will never have the dignity to die at the hands of the elves. I will wither away here in my magic prison, a puppet of the queen's to upset whoever she bunks me with until The End of Planes."

Cole sat up on his cot and smacked his dry tongue against the roof of his mouth. His eyes softened with curiosity.

"Don't you see, Cole? *I* was meant to upset *you*. And I have. Something the queen would view as a victory." His eyes narrowed. "That, I cannot abide. And so, I apologize."

Cole weakly pushed himself to his feet. He approached the bars of the magic mirror and stared into the eyes of his cellmate. The old man looked remorseful but dignified. Cole couldn't help but respect the man. They said nothing to each other, but Cole ate that day.

The next week passed peacefully. Cole ate regularly again and his congenial mood recovered. Il i'Tir still felt remorseful and indulged Cole by listening to his stories. Cole shared with Il i'Tir all his fondest memories, most wild exploits, and deepest secrets. The warlock took these to heart and offered a cautious, but always favorable, opinion.

"You know all there is to know about me and my heroic deeds, why don't you tell me some of yours?"

"Warlocks are generally not considered heroes."

"According to who? Elves? What do those judgmental jerks know anyway? I'm sure you've done something heroic in your life."

Il i'Tir stroked his hairless chin, thinking of a good example.

"Oh! I know!" Cole shouted and bounced excited as a child during their favorite bedtime story. "Tell me how you defeated the treacherous elven king to save your daughter."

A sinister grin crept up the corners of Il i'Tir's mouth. "Gladly."

Cole sat cross-legged on the floor in front of the magic mirror. Il i'Tir described the events leading to the elven king's death.

"Some time ago, I cannot tell you how long, as I have lost track of time since I came to be stuck in this dreadful mirror, but some time ago...

"It came to my attention that an evil dragon named Hexor sought to bring about the genocide of all living beings nondragon. In his twisted point of view, dragons are the only race worthy of the world. A similar opinion the elves have of humans."

Cole nodded, his brow etched with concern. As horrible as the elves are, he thought this dragon must be ten times worse. To want to kill all living beings was pure evil. He wondered if Hexor was the same dragon that captured Princess Oriel but allowed the warlock to continue.

"Rumors of other dragons migrating to the Hexor's volcano fortress spread. Using an orb I was able to scry, what you may call view from afar, and see this was more than rumor; it was the truth. A confederacy of dragons led by Hexor was hellbent on carrying out this nightmare scenario of restoring the world for dragons. I had to stop them.

"Eld's resources were already divided among the existing nations. So I laid claim to a small kingdom abandoned within Elfwood. There are so many untapped resources in this plane; it would be foolish not to use them against Hexor.

"My claim upset the elven king greatly. Long ago the elves took their ancient knowledge to this magical plane. They wanted to keep their secrets from humans. The elven king did not even have the civility to discuss my claim face to face. He sent a messenger, a lowly general, who ordered me to leave Elfwood and never return."

"What did you do?" Cole asked, his eyes alight with interest.

"I killed the messenger. Sent his head in a basket back to the elves and waited for his response."

"Wow! I'd say you made your message loud and clear."

"Indeed. The elven king gathered his army and invaded my new kingdom. I was forced to assemble an army of my own. Besides my daughter Tara, a powerful warrior in her own right, all I could recruit was the other rejected race of Elfwood: goblins."

"Goblins?!"

"I was in a desperate situation, Cole. Against an army of elves one thousand strong, I needed all the support I could get."

Il i'Tir's pleading eyes calmed Cole. Sure, Cole hated goblins, but he decided he hated elves even more and forgave Il i'Tir's desperate pact. He apologized for his shortsightedness and begged the warlock to continue.

"The day the elven king died, the armies of elves and goblins faced one another on two opposing hills. Only a small valley separated our forces. The sun shined behind the arrogant elven army. Their dull green banners flickered behind them, mocking my flagless goblins. A crescent moon hung proudly in the starry night behind me and my daughter. Commanders of one hundred thousand goblins, we were not to be taken lightly. The sky above the valley below us blended dusk and dawn into a marigold and wine sea of clouds. It was a perfect day to war.

"The elves stared at us with their usual smug silence in full-blown force. I turned to my daughter Tara, her exquisite face shielded by a black helm sculpted like a Minotaur. Her black polished plate mail craved to be soiled by the blood of elves."

Breathless, Cole said, "I'm sure she made her father proud that day."

"She did," Il i'Tir said and dabbed a tear from the corner of his eye. "She's intimidating; gets it from me. Tara carried a razor sharp boomerang holstered to her belt. I caught her absentmindedly fondling it as she waited to battle, mounted on her freybug, Trux."

"What's a freybug?"

"A monstrous black dog with the ears of a bat, fangs of a tiger, and a body as big as a bull. Tara rode the beast bareback, gripping its fur as her reigns."

Cole shuddered with joy. "Go on."

"On the opposing hill, another father and daughter pair prepared for battle. Domina, captain of the elven rangers, and her father, the self-righteous King Pa-Kota. A hulk of muscle, he stood seven feet tall, three feet taller than an average elf. His silver shoulder length hair blew out behind him like a cape. He wore no armor, but I detected he was protected by magical war paint. It infused his body with strength and agility. He gripped a spear in his left hand and a griffin feather in his right; a token of affection from his beloved wife, the elven queen.

"Domina looked to her father for a blessing before the battle. The most affection he could muster was a distant nod of approval. The elven king ceremoniously kissed the griffin feather and stuck it in his chaplet.

"Domina turned to her rangers and pursed her lips, pleased with their composure. She glanced at my goblins and scoffed at their inability to hold ranks. I could see in her eyes she thought this would be an easy victory.

"She could not have been more wrong."

His breath short and fast, Cole leaned forward and sat on the edge of his cot, captivated by the warlock's tale.

"At the sound of a horn, my goblin army charged into battle. The elven king held his ranks, determined to maintain the high ground. Let him have it, thought I. He had the high ground, but I had the numbers.

"One hundred thousand goblins charged uphill and were greeted by volleys of arrows. The lucky few who survived were cut down by the front line of rangers wielding dual swords. It seemed as if we were weak, but that's what I wanted the elves to think.

"My daughter Tara looked to me, but I didn't need to give her the command. She spurred her freybug and rode into battle!"

Cole caught his breath. Who was this war-maiden? And why did the simple thought of her make his stomach clench with excitement? He felt like those silly girls back home, the ones you found in any tavern in Flounder, who gushed and sighed over the schmaltzy and romantic tales sung by traveling bards. Cole listened, transfixed by the warlock's story of his daughter.

"Seven times upon her ascent uphill, she threw her boomerang blade and severed elven heads from their shoulders. Tara tore through their ranks, slaying elves; my angel of death." Il i'Tir smiled fondly, recalling his daughter's might. "It was she who swayed the battle in my favor.

"Domina battled a cluster of goblins. She heard a whirring sound and instinctively ducked. If she had not, she would have lost her head that day. The elven ranger behind her was decapitated, a cold reminder of my baby's ferocity.

"An elven captain looked up at Tara mounted on her freybug, clad in pitch black armor. She charged at her with the sole intention of killing her. Even for an elf, I was shocked Domina was dexterous enough to tumble aside and out of harm's way.

"The cursed elf slashed at the legs of Tara's freybug. Tara was thrown off her howling giant dog and landed face first in a pile of elf and goblin corpses. She stood and braced herself for battle; one princess against another.

"They proved evenly matched, but with different talents. Domina attacked with precision and Tara used her brute strength to defend herself."

Cole's mouth fell open. He could barely contain his excitement.

Il i'Tir said with great fervor, "A heavy backhanded blow later, Domina was on her back, her swords cast aside. The crushing truth of her imminent death weighed down on her. Triumphant, my daughter stood above the panicked elf, ready to drive the life from her body.

"Tara looked across the battlefield to me, and I imagine, behind her helmet, she smiled. You can guess how proud I was. Father of the elf slayer."

Cole sighed. She was perfect.

"On my command, Tara brought her boomerang blade down on the elf. Domina raised her arms, a futile defense, but instinct knows not reason."

"But that doesn't make sense. Domina's alive. Tara couldn't have killed her."

"She didn't," the warlock said sullen. "Tara's blade met the long ironwood spear of the elven king. The weapons rang across the battlefield, alerting me to the seriousness my baby's trouble. From my dark hill, I watched my daughter struggle to defend herself. The elven king overwhelmed her with his superior spearplay."

Cole brought his fingers to his mouth and bit them, trying to contain his fright.

"Tara blocked attack after attack, but was driven back into the ranks of the remaining elven rangers. I leaped into action. I whispered dark magical words, a hex to suck the life-strength out of my remaining goblins. They clasped their tiny clawed hands over their necks and choked on the malevolent spell. I drained their life force and increased my strength tenfold.

"I dissipated into a purple mist and wafted across the battlefield, killing all the elves I passed like a plague. When I reappeared behind the elven king, I blasted him with dark matter. The spell corrupted the purity of his soul and ate his spirit. He fell, in a most undignified manner, face first into the blood soaked grass. The king of Elfwood was dead."

Cole gasped in awed horror at the warlock. *How on earth did the elves ever capture someone so powerful?* he wondered.

"The sole elf remaining on the battlefield was Domina. She stared, heartbroken as her father withered before her. The hex consumed his soul and feasted on his flesh. She screamed until her voice was hoarse and called for reinforcements hiding in the trees. The reinforcements stormed out of the woods and sprinted to Domina's aid, led by her mother, Queen Jenera.

"I knew time was scarce and helped Tara to her feet, and much to her protest, urged her to flee while I protected her escape. And as soon as my daughter was safe and out of sight, I surrendered to the remaining elves. I depleted my power to defeat the elven king. It would have been suicide to continue.

"Like you I was not given a fair trial, and sentenced to life imprisonment by the vengeful queen. Using a magical artifact from the sylvans, they trapped me in this mirror and the rest, as they say, is history."

Cole contemplated the tale. His hatred for the elves burned hotter than ever. Without a word, he stood, stretched, and began a set of push-ups.

"Something wrong?" Il i'Tir asked.

"I have to get you out of here," Cole said between repetitions. "Your daughter needs you."

"And exercise is the answer?"

"The only way I can save you and defeat the elves is if I become a master warrior. If I want to become a master warrior, I have to train my butt off. I've wasted too much time feeling sorry for myself."

"There is another way," Il i'Tir said. "But it's probably too dangerous for you."

Cole stopped mid-push-up, stood, and walked up to the mirror, determined to do anything to help. "Tell me," he said.

Il i'Tir stood and walked to the mirror glass. He looked over his shoulders as if someone may be listening and then back at Cole. "I could make you the most powerful warrior the world has ever known," he whispered. "All I need is a bit of magic."

"Great," Cole said, "but I don't know any magic. How am I supposed to help?"

"I am a warlock. My magic comes from the pacts I make."

"Well, sign me up," Cole said with a smile.

"Excellent. Swear your allegiance to me with your blood."

"You're not a vampire are you?"

"No. I am much more powerful."

CHAPTER TWENTY-THREE

Escape from Elfwick

The elves led Pal and Hikari to the massive tree fortress past the small village at its base. Smithies, artisans, and townsfolk stopped their daily business to get a look at the humans. A few mischievous elven children picked up rocks and threw them at the prisoners. A sharp edged rock scraped the side of Pal's temple, a trickle of blood dripping down his cheekbone. Domina wheeled on the children and admonished them for such ignoble behavior.

"You brats act as low as humans!"

The children's tall pointy ears drooped and they ran away in shame.

"Thank you," Pal said.

"Keep walking, human," Domina said as she passed.

Pal observed her athletic figure, her mocha hair braided in intricate elven weaves, and her heartbreaking azure eyes.

"You're staring," Domina said, as sharp a nail.

"Forgive me. If you weren't trying to walk so close to me, I wouldn't worry you may try to kill me again."

"I am not trying to walk close to you," she said and scowled.

"You're getting closer by the second," Pal whispered.

"All humans are alike. Vulgar and disrespectful."

"Not all humans. Just me," Pal said and flashed a smile.

Domina rolled her eyes. Sickened by the human, she decided to take point and quickened her pace. Pal watched her hustle all the way to the front of the line. When she was out of sight, he rubbed his raw and bloody wrists against the ropes binding him. The bloody trail he left for the Locksmiths to follow continued.

Domina led Hikari and Pal into the courtroom for judgment. Elven courtiers whispered among themselves. The elven queen sat on her pinecone throne as regal and poised as a cat, appraising her new prisoners. "A paladin? I thought your kind was extinct."

"There are still a few of us," Hikari said.

"Who is your cleric?" the elven queen asked.

"I have no cleric," Hikari said.

"A fallen paladin in my court. What an honor," the elven queen said, mocking Hikari.

The court hissed with laughter.

Domina stepped forward and addressed her mother. "They traveled with the unicorn murderer."

The laughter in the court ceased. The elven queen burned with anger.

"Accomplices?!"

"Your highness," Hikari said. "Please enlighten me about what you accuse us of."

The elven queen raised the bone white spiral grooved horn and held it out for Hikari, Pal, and the entire court to see.

"Do you not recognize this?" she bellowed.

"I recognize it is a unicorn's horn, but I have never seen it before in my life."

"Lies!"

"A paladin never lies."

"Yes, but you are a fallen paladin. How could I trust you? If an elf were to lie, to corrupt her own purity, her skin would turn black as pitch and all would see and know she is untrue. When humans lie, which they seem to do daily, they continue unmarked. It is as if it is a human's very nature to be deceitful."

"I may no longer serve a cleric but my master has and always will be Rey, the light of our sky, who warms Mud'hir Erta and shines on her children with favor." Hikari presented his sword and knelt. "I swear by my sword and Rey's name that I tell you true."

Hundreds of feet below the courtroom, Cole and Il i'Tir set into motion their escape. Cole stuck his index finger into his mouth and bit until the metallic taste of blood reached his tongue.

"Place your finger on the mirror," the warlock said from within.

Without his meager prison diet, Cole never would have fit his hands through the narrow bars encasing the magic mirror. A line of blood streaked down the cold glass of the mirror. What happened next shocked Cole. Il i'Tir kissed the mirror and somehow sucked Cole's blood through it. Cole felt searing pain rush from his finger up to his shoulder until it overtook him completely. He wailed in agony.

Outside the cell, the warden dropped his bottle of mead. He shared a distressed look with his deputy, who was about to turn over the minute glass.

The last sip of blood was sucked from his body, and Cole collapsed.

Il i'Tir took a deep breath. His old withered face looked twenty years younger. Color returned to his pale skin. His eyes glowed with dark magic. Cole's blood was more potent than the warlock imagined. Dark power coursed through Il i'Tir; he was fully regenerated.

Outside the cell, the warden looked to his deputy. "Don't stand there, do something!"

The deputy ripped the ring of keys from his belt and unlocked the door. The warden drew his sword, handed the deputy a lantern, and the deputy entered the room holding it out in front of him. Searching the room, he found Cole's pale body in a heap on the floor.

"He's dead!" the deputy shouted. "The unicorn killer is dead!"

The warden entered the room cautiously. The deputy set the lantern down and examined Cole's body. There was no pulse and his purple skin felt waxy.

Brandishing his ironwood sword, the warden rushed to the mirror. "What have you done to him, warlock?"

Il i'Tir replied with a cold soulless smile.

"Answer me!"

The deputy joined the warden in front of the mirror and said, "We should alert the queen."

Il i'Tir's eyes burned violet. "How will you do that?" he asked.

The guards blinked and found themselves trapped in the mirror.

Il i'Tir stood where they once were. "...when you're stuck in there?"

The guards pounded on the glass. They cried for help, but it was useless.

Il i'Tir approached the mirror. "I've been waiting to do this for a long, long time," he said and raised his hand.

The guards clung to each other.

The warlock reached through the bars and straightened the magic mirror. Just a smidge. Perfect. He sighed in relief. The slightly crooked mirror had tortured the obsessive compulsive warlock for decades. Things were finally looking up.

Il i'Tir turned to Cole and said, "Rise."

A violet vapor enveloped Cole. The warlock transformed him into a muscle-bound juggernaut of a man. His eyelids blinked open. And under them, two pitch black chasms without fear, remorse, or pity. Filled with unnatural strength, he rose to his feet. Cole flexed his immense muscles, turned to the wall, and punched his fist through the rock.

Il i'Tir patted Cole's mammoth shoulder and said, "Time to play."

In the courtroom above, Hikari had had enough of the elven queen's relentless interrogation. "Your highness, I beg you release us and our companion. We are on an important mission."

"What mission?" the elven queen asked.

"To rescue King Langsley's missing daughter, Princess Oriel."

"Langsley? Is that old goat still alive?"

"We mean no harm to you or any of the Fair Folk," Hikari said. "There has been a misunderstanding."

"Misunderstanding?"

The elven queen laughed, a condemnatory breath, and the court joined her. Pal had only been on trial once before during his sailing days. The lawmen prosecuting him and the other pirates had more compassion than the elves. Hikari took a deep breath and collected his composure.

"We found goblin corpses outside the Elfwood gate," he said. "Perhaps Cole defended the unicorn and was mistaken for its killer."

The elven queen pondered the paladin's supposition for a moment and read the honesty in his eyes. "You never said anything about goblins, Domina."

"You know all too well, Mother, humans will align themselves with any monster if it serves their purpose."

"For an elf who has probably never left Elfwood, you sure seem to know a lot about humans," Pal said.

"You're all the same."

"Not true. Want me to prove it?"

"I don't want anything from you."

"Sure you don't," Pal said and winked at Domina.

She opened her mouth, and when nothing came out, turned her eyes to the floor.

"Perhaps Cole can clear this matter up for us," Hikari said. "If he is guilty, we'll leave him in your custody. If not..." Hikari stepped forward, holding the rope that had bound his wrist. "We would like to be on our way."

Twenty elven swords rushed to Hikari's throat.

"As you can see," Hikari said, "if I wanted to escape, I could have done so long ago."

Pal looked at him in disbelief and said, "That would have been nice to know before we made the long journey here."

"But I tied those knots myself," a strapping young ranger claimed.

"Nothing can bind the words of truth," Hikari said.

The elven queen stood, silencing the court, and addressed Hikari. "Let's see what your friend Cole has to say for himself."

The steel door of what used to be Il i'Tir and Cole's cell exploded off its hinges. Elven guards ran down the hallway to investigate. They waved their hands and coughed, rushing into the dusty corridor. The dust settled and Cole stood in the door frame, Il i'Tir behind him.

One of the guards shouted, "Il i'Tir has escaped!"

Il i'Tir whispered into Cole's ear, "Time to test your new powers."

Cole smiled. His vacant black eyes showed no remorse. Using his corrupt super strength, he fought the elven guards barehanded. Armed, they were no match for him. They waved their swords and poked at him with their ironwood polearms. Cole laughed and slapped away their weapons with the strength of a rhino. Cole kicked a guard into a group of advancing elves and bowled them over. He punched another elf out of his boots. He ripped up the floorboards and pulled them out from under a new group of guards like a carpet. Il i'Tir followed Cole's path of destruction. He finished off each elf with a deadly life stealing hex, and with each life he took, the warlock's power grew.

The elven queen and her escorts, Domina, Hikari, and Pal descended into the dungeons. An elven guard thrown across the hallway landed at the elven queen's feet. She looked down the hallway in horror.

"What madness is this?" she asked.

Cole charged into sight and battered another group of guards with the bars of an empty cell.

Hikari stood aghast in front of the elven queen. "Cole?"

Cole panted like someone caught between waking and a nightmare. "Hikari?" he spoke in a deep and distant voice.

Il i'Tir stepped in front of Cole and addressed the elven queen. "I told you Jenera, you should have killed me when you had the chance."

Il i'Tir spread his arms and transformed into a massive green dragon. The behemoth's thick scaly hide glistened. They were emeralds in the candlelight and cast glittering reflections about the dungeon. His horned skull plate stretched from his forehead like a triceratops. Two folded leathery wings rested on his back. So close to the dragon, Cole saw freckles of tiny brown spikes on his hide. He stared at the dark brown horn jutting up from his nose. Snorting and sniffing, the dragon's giant nostrils pulsed as he inhaled the scents in the room. A dull sense of fear in the air intoxicated him. The green dragon grinned. Row after row of calcium daggers filled his mouth, large enough to eat an elf guard in one gulp. Which he did.

After his long overdue meal, Il i'Tir displayed his powerful wings. He flexed his massive arms and flaunted his razor sharp claws. His tail danced behind him, a cobra waiting to strike. He lowered his frilled head and locked his yellow eyes with all occupying the hallway. The green dragon's petrifying glare stunned everyone just long enough for him to charge.

The dragon shoveled the elven escorts and guards away with its head. He swatted Hikari and the elven queen aside, mere flies compared to his powerful tail. He roared and spewed a thick poisonous gas from his mouth.

The enormous dark cloud billowed toward Domina but Pal dove in front of her and pushed her to safety. She landed hard on the floor, bruising her tailbone, and a shockwave of pain shot up her spine. Through tears, she watched Pal disappear into the fog of the dragon's poisonous breath.

Overwhelmed with unexpected concern, Domina filled her lungs with clean air and dashed into the mist. Blind, she flailed her hands until her fingers found a strong muscular back. She tightened her grip around the cloth of his shirt and pulled Pal out of the fog. Mucus oozed from his mouth, nose, and eyes. She dragged him up the stairs and out of the dungeons to safety.

Cole rubbed his eyes and blinked, fighting the dulling effects of the hex Il i'Tir placed on him.

"Stop," he shouted. "You're hurting my friends!"

"*I* am your friend," the green dragon replied.

Cole hesitated. Battling the hex with his will, his moral code began to recover.

The dragon gently laid a claw on Cole's shoulder. "Come with me, Cole. You have so much potential. Join me on my quest. Together, nothing can stop us."

Cole looked at his fallen friends and asked, "What have I done?"

"They left you in that prison to rot," the dragon said. "I made you powerful. Think of what you'll accomplish at my side. You can have treasure beyond your wildest imagination. Everyone will know your name, Cole. And they will fear you."

"I don't want to be feared."

The dragon's yellow eyes turned to slits. He shook his head with disappointment and said, "So be it."

The dragon plunged a claw into Cole's chest. He drained him of all his superpowers so his bulging biceps and swollen chest shrunk. His stretched clothes wilted around his malnourished body. He gaped, staring into the dragon's open mouth. Overwhelming fear of his imminent death took control of him.

Hikari flew through the air, propelled by the divine power of the Sun Sword. He slashed the dragon across his snout, cutting the horn from his nose. The dragon stumbled into a wall, shaking the foundations of the dungeons.

Cole fell back into Hikari's arms. He looked into his friend's eyes with thanks and guilt. Had the dragon drained him completely, he would have died.

"Hikari," Cole said.

"Now is not the time for apologies."

The green dragon covered his bleeding nose with his claws and roared, spitting acid in the air.

Hikari leveled the tip of his glowing katana at the green dragon's heart and shouted, "Be gone, monster!"

"A paladin?" the dragon snarled in disbelief.

Hikari stepped in front of Cole and said, "You shall not harm this one."

The dragon opened his mouth wide and unleashed poisonous gas. Hikari closed his eyes. An aura of blinding light shielded him and Cole from the breath's poisonous effects.

"Your poison cannot harm me," Hikari said, weakened by the energy he expended to protect himself and Cole.

The dragon roared, spun, and flogged Hikari with his spiked tail. Hikari crashed into the wall at the end of the hallway and fell unconscious in a heap of chainmail.

"Hikari!" Cole shouted and rushed to his side.

The dragon planted a scaly leg in front of his former cellmate to block his path. "Now you will suffer the same fate as your friends."

More poisonous gas billowed from the dragon's nostrils. Cole wanted to attack, but the green dragon's hypnotizing eyes crippled him with fear. The only thing he could do was hold his breath against the deadly fog.

Macario inexplicably appeared out of thin air. He plugged one of Il i'Tir's nostrils with pieces of broken floorboard. The dragon's sneeze imploded and burst his eardrums. His entire skull throbbed in agony. Il i'Tir roared and writhed in pain, clawing the wood from his nose. Staggering, coughing, and unable to breathe or see, the dragon retreated. He burst through the ceiling and tunneled a desperate escape route. Not a minute later, he surfaced at the base of Elfwick, scattering unlucky elves who happened to be there. The Emerald Enormity roared at the stunned villagers. He whipped a dozen centaurs with his tail, and bounded away to its secret lair, devastating much of the village in its wake.

Below in the dungeon, the ceiling caved in and guards escorted the elven queen to safety. Hikari stood, weakened by his fall and Cole rubbed his eyes, not believing he was still alive. Nor could he believe Macario's appearance.

"That was close," Macario said, and spotting something on the floor, bent down, and picked up the dragon horn. "Finders keepers."

CHAPTER TWENTY-FOUR

Parting Gifts

Pal woke in a bed of needle leaves in the center of a nest, built on one of Elfwick's branches. He had no idea how he got there, or why his entire skeleton felt brittle. All he knew was he was not alone. Macario and Cole chattered away. Another one of their annoying conversations about magic spells and other arcane nonsense.

"Can't a guy get any peace and quiet around here?" Pal asked, silencing them...for a second.

They pounced into bed with Pal, and needle leaves flew like confetti. Cole and Macario laughed and cheered. They clung to their irritated friend, who thought if they hugged him any tighter he may snap.

"How are you feeling, Pal?" Cole asked.

"Awful. Let me go, you idiots."

The pair released Pal.

"You almost died," Macario said.

"I know," Pal said. "Where were you, Macario? I thought you were supposed to save my life."

"I did save your life," Macario explained. "Before the elves captured you and Hikari, I shrank to the size of an ant and hid in one of your pockets. I noticed that you left a trail of blood for me to follow so I could rescue you. A rather dramatic course of action I must admit, but creative considering the circumstances. When we arrived at Elfwick, I watched your trial, which I found entertaining although unfair. Finally, I followed you to the dungeons where we reunited with Cole. You can imagine my surprise when I found out Cole allied with an evil warlock who turned out to be a dragon in disguise. That's when I felt it appropriate to reveal myself and come to your aid."

"I'm so glad you felt it was appropriate to reveal yourself after the dragon blasted me with his breath. That doesn't count as paying off your life debt. You still owe me."

Macario scratched his chin and said, "I suppose you could argue, technically, that I saved Cole's life."

Pal squinted at Cole. "You look terrible."

The youth who was as large and thick as an ox was now an emaciated shadow of his former self. In fact, he looked a hundred pounds lighter since the day before. Cole nervously combed his hand through his long beard. "I was locked in that dungeon for almost four years."

"No. It was only a single day," Macario reminded him. "The magic cell extends time within."

"Well, it felt like forever to me."

Pal took Cole's hand. "I bet. I spent a few months in prison once. Worst days of my life."

"When were you in prison?" Cole asked.

"It's a long story. Get a haircut and something to eat. Looking at you makes me hungry."

Cole forced a smile. "Okay." He was traumatized by the ordeal but buried his pain deep inside himself.

The last person Pal wanted to see climbed into the nest with a bowl of water and a rag.

"What's she doing here?" Pal asked.

Domina bit her lip and repeated her internal mantra as she approached the bed. *Don't kill the human. Don't kill the human. Don't kill...*

"Easy, Pal. Domina rescued you from the dragon's breath. Without her medicines, you would have been a goner," Cole said.

Domina knelt by Pal, set the bowl beside her, and took a small pouch from her belt. "I came to check up on you. While you slept, I cured you of the toxins in your system."

"What's that?" Pal asked.

"Medicine," Domina said, opened her purse, and sprinkled herbs and powders into the bowl of water. She mixed the ingredients with her hands, tracing figure eights with her nails on the bottom of the wood bowl.

Hypnotized by the aroma of springtime, Pal reclined on the bed, the hint of a smile on his face. Domina dipped the rag into the bowl and applied the salve to Pal's forehead. She warmed his aching temples, massaged his clogged sinuses, and rubbed his stiff neck. Pal could swear the last of the awful aches and pains left his body under her touch.

Cole and Macario shared a knowing look.

"You know, Pal," Cole said, "these elves aren't as bad as they seem. Sure, they're arrogant, stubborn, and..." Domina glared at Cole. "...extremely forgiving. I mean, look at this great outfit they gave me." He spun in a circle, showing off the camouflaged garb given to him by the rangers.

Domina turned her attention back to her patient. She unbuttoned Pal's shirt. His tanned skin returned to its natural color. "On behalf of my queen, I apologize for our inhospitality."

"What about on your behalf?" he asked. "Do you apologize for kidnapping me?"

"I saved your life."

"And you nearly killed me!"

Macario leaned over to Cole and said, "Let's leave the lovers to quarrel."

"We are not lovers!" Domina and Pal shouted in unison.

Elsewhere in Elfwick, Hikari stood in the war room built in a hollow of the tree. The floor beneath his feet smelled of freshly cut grass and wood chips. He walked in a circle around a large wooden table, studying maps of Elfwood. The elven queen and her generals sat around the table. They wore ceremonial war paint, feathers, animal furs, teeth, and horns.

The stout general of artillery wore a Sasquatch tunic and a single pegasus downright feather in his hair. He pointed to one of the ancient maps rolled out on the tabletop. "The elven king, Pa-Kota, Mud'hir rest his spirit, last fought Il i'Tir, in Twilight Valley near the Rainbow Falls."

Hikari nodded, trying to keep up with the shifting images on the Elfwood maps.

"Therein lies the Pixie Caves, and beyond that no elf has set foot. It could possibly be the warlock's lair."

The young infantry general wore a jackalope hood and an upright pegasus feather. "Now that we know what the warlock truly is, we also know what his daughter is. A half-dragon. Halflings are an unpredictable breed. You never know what powers they will inherit from their parents. A half-dragon may grow wings or tails or claws. Others will look human but wield dragon powers such as strength and cunning. Until they reveal themselves, you don't know what you are up against."

"Do I have to worry about any other dragons occupying Elfwood?" Hikari asked.

The highest ranking general, an elf with excellent posture and a magnificent necklace of hippogriff talons around his long thick neck, turned to the paladin. His expression was grave. "Not a single dragon has set foot in Elfwood until Il i'Tir stole his way into our peaceful realm. He crossed through the gate to Elfwood using Princess Oriel's innocence as his key."

"The truth is, we'd heard rumors of a dragon, the Emerald Enormity," the queen said. "But my husband paid no heed to them. He believed...we all believed Il i'Tir to be another greedy human. The misconception cost my husband his life."

Hikari bowed to the queen. "I vow by my blade, we will avenge your husband and bring this Emerald Enormity to justice."

The next morning, the court was crowded. Elven soldiers and rangers dressed in celebratory garb stood in ranks. Courtiers squeezed as close to the throne steps as possible. Druids clung to the walls and tried to remain out of sight. The villagers who weren't burying their dead came to see the heroes off.

The elven queen and her daughter sat on their pinecone thrones. Jenera wore a gown of billowing orange silks, and Domina, her camouflage ranger outfit. Her bored expression gave away her longing to be lost in the crowd. She did not want to be up on a pedestal for all to look at. Especially the no good rascal human who went by the ridiculous name of Pal.

A hush fell over the crowd as Cole (freshly shaved and trimmed), Hikari, Pal, and Macario entered the courtroom. Cole laughed to himself. He thought, *yesterday, the elves wanted to kill me. Today they're throwing me a going away party.*

The quartet stood before the queen. She rose to her feet and the court hushed. "My people have underestimated you," she began. "We were quick to judgment. Mud'hir Erta frowns upon us for our short-sightedness. Those who judge blindly cannot see the truth. There is purity in your hearts. You are proof of humankind's potential to bring good back into the world. Please accept these gifts as our humble apology."

The queen turned and three of her female attendants stepped forward, each bearing a gift. The first was a tall, thin, and twisted staff carved from a branch of a rowan tree.

"Macario," she said. "Your cunning use of magic defeated Il i'Tir once, but he won't be surprised again. I give you the Sylvanus Staff. A gift from our cousins, the high elves. My people know not of their arcane ways and so I pass it on to you. May you channel its deep pool of mana to bolster your spells."

Macario bowed and accepted the staff. It fit well in his hands, light of weight and thin in circumference, with knots of wood signifying a point of grip. Macario grinned, although he felt like striking out in a traditional Maji Tribe jubilant dance.

"Hikari Musha," the elven queen said with a smile, "What do I give to a paladin?"

Hikari bent down on one knee and said, "No gift is necessary your highness."

"And yet I have one for you," she said and gifted Hikari a beaded necklace with a wooden pendant of the planet. "The Amulet of Mud'hir Erta. Your god, Rey shines down on Mud'hir, feeding her growth. Your wisdom has shone upon me and I have grown. May this holy symbol stand for our alliance. Sun and earth. Man and elf."

Hikari bowed his head and the queen's attendant slipped the beaded necklace over his head. It fell and clinked against his golden chainmail jacket. The amulet was a wooden coin inlaid with a golden icon of Elfwick. Although his heart lay in Rey's hands, he felt the intrinsic energy of Mud'hir Erta emanating from the amulet.

The queen took the third gift from the last attendant. "Cole," she said.

Cole's heart raced in his chest. The anticipation killed him. Whatever his gift was, it was small enough to fit in her palm. Was it a ring? Some extraordinary ring of power? A flying ring? A super-speed ring? Maybe it wasn't a ring at all. It could be a brooch. Were brooches still in fashion? Who cares, as long as it's powerful!

"Please accept this seed of hope." The queen dropped a small ordinary looking seed the size of a walnut into the palm of Cole's hand. The court gasped at the queen's generosity. Cole didn't get it. It was only a seed. It felt rough and sprouted straggling fibrous hairs. "Plant a seed, nurture it, give it time, and one day, it will blossom."

Cole looked at the stupid little seed in his hand and thought, *Macario got a magic staff. Hikari got an awesome amulet. And all I get is a stupid seed?!* He barely managed to mask his disappointment and thanked the queen for the worst gift in the world. He shoved the seed into his pocket and tried to forget it was there.

"And you," the queen addressed Pal. "My daughter has cured you of the dragon's poisonous breath. You have been given a second chance. Do not squander it."

Pal forced a smile and mock-bowed for the queen.

The queen sat back on her throne and said, "My last gift is more of a loan. The lands of Elfwood are hard to navigate for those who are not born Fair Folk. My daughter Domina will guide you to the Rainbow Falls. She is the kingdom's most skilled ranger."

"But, mother..."

"I have spoken."

All present bowed to the queen and ushered out of the court.

As Macario crossed the threshold of the main doors, he asked Cole, "What's the matter, my friend?"

Cole whispered, "A stupid seed?!"

"It's symbolic."

"I'd rather have a symbolic sword."

When Domina was alone with her mother she said, "I don't want to go."

"You don't have a choice. Do you think I can place the fate of our kingdom in human hands alone? You will aid them on their quest, but do not engage the dragon. If he attacks, I want you to turn and run as fast as possible. You must survive. No matter what, my daughter. Survive."

Domina felt her mother press a griffin feather into her hand. Specks of her father's blood ran up its vane. The harsh memory of her father's death coursed through her. She kissed it and proudly placed it in her hair. "I will return, mother."

The elven queen nodded and left the court. Domina sank into her throne. Excited at her chance for revenge, but plagued with an unfamiliar nervousness. To be on a quest with that incorrigible human gave her a pin prickly feeling in her heart. Her sigh echoed throughout the court. She calmed herself by contemplating what weapons to pack.

CHAPTER TWENTY-FIVE

Homecoming

Weak and ailing, Il i'Tir flew with effort to the center of a briar labyrinth, toward his bramble tower. Surrounding his lair were the goblin breeding grounds to the south, the sylvan camp to the west, the armories and goblin barracks to the north, and stables to the east. Sylvan smithies halted their production of magically infused weapons and armor. Horns blew and they fell in line to greet the Emerald Enormity.

Masses of goblins and hobgoblins gathered at the base of the bramble tower, cheering their king's return. The dragon crash-landed in front of his army. He kicked up a wave of dirt, knocking down twenty goblins. Beside the rowdy goblins, ranks of sylvan battalions assembled in crisp formation. The sylvan had similar physiques to their elven cousins, but their skin was snow white and their hair platinum blond. They wore masterwork armor, forged with magical enhancements, rivaled by no race but the dwarfs. They carried heavy shields and longswords. On their breastplates, they bore the crest of a green dragon. Emotionless and brilliant, the Fair Folk warriors were Il i'Tir's most important commodity.

That is, except for Tara, his deadly half-dragon daughter. Her face was hidden behind her pitch-black Minotaur helmet. She gripped her trusty boomerang blade holstered in her belt.

Il i'Tir allowed his daughter to approach and she knelt at his enormous clawed foot. "Welcome home, father," she said.

"Rise, my daughter." The dragon lifted his frilled head high, and spoke to his army. "For too long, I was wrongfully imprisoned by the elves because they refuse to share the wealth of these lands. They who are so few, but who have so much, reap the fruits of the land. And we, the monsters who outnumber them one ninety-nine to one, are never given our fair share. If they will not give us our gods-given rights of wealth and land and freedom, we must take them!"

The goblin multitude hollered with excitement. Even though the speech was a little long for most of the goblins' attention spans, they still liked the inspirational tone of voice the scary dragon used. They raised their axes and swords and maces and crossbows into the air and cheered when he stopped talking. The high elves stood at attention and emotionless, waiting for Il i'Tir to continue.

"Hexor assembles his Legions of Dread, ten thousand strong. I have bred over a hundred thousand goblins and gained the support of the sylvan nation. But how am I supposed to stop the Crimson Nemesis from his apocalyptic plot if the elves stand in my path?"

Tara stepped forward. "Father, I apologize. Our defeat at Twilight Valley depleted our entire army. I planned to organize a rescue party, but the sylvan will not take arms against the elves."

"Is that true?" Il i'Tir snarled.

Adrias, a sylvan lieutenant, spoke for his people. "We fight against the Crimson Nemesis, not the elves. We made clear our terms when we signed your pact."

"That they were," the dragon agreed. "But if we are met again with hostility in our pursuit to save the world, will you fight, or will you let the elves secure Hexor's victory?"

Adrias maintained his impassive expression. "We shall do what is necessary."

"I hope so. I hope so," the dragon repeated to emphasize his frustration. "How long was I trapped in that wretched prison?"

"One moon," Tara said.

Il i'Tir closed his eyes. Barely any time had passed for Tara but more than a century of his life, stolen from him. It was nearly impossible to maintain composure in front of his troops, but he was their savior. He needed to be strong for them. For the cause.

His eyes opened, frightening and determined to get revenge, he focused them past his daughter. "One moon to you but a lifetime to me."

Tara hung her head, shamed.

"Goblins! If you serve me, all goblin kind will prevail. Goblins will finally earn their fair share. And it will be because of your heroics. Do I have your allegiance?"

The goblins cheered.

"Excellent," Il i'Tir said.

He uttered dark words invoking one of the most horrible warlock spells. He raised his claw and stripped the souls from every goblin and hobgoblin in assembly. Their lifeless bodies collapsed and their energy swirled in a malevolent vortex Il i'Tir reshaped for darker means. He corrupted their spirits and transformed them into nightmarish ghosts called wraiths.

Tara and the sylvan ranks faltered in their haunting presence.

In the foul tongue, the Emerald Enormity whispered instructions to the ethereal army of wraiths. Their mission; to rampage all living creatures of the Elfwood, and cast a cloud of despair over his enemies. They ran through the labyrinth, phasing through the briar walls and left a trail of hate and anxiety in their wake.

Tara looked up into her father's unforgiving yellow eyes.

"Breed more goblins. I must rest and regenerate."

The dragon curled his wings and shifted into his human form. Two sylvan guards opened the tower doors for the warlock. He climbed the thousand steps to the top of his tower where he intended to feast on Princess Oriel's royal blood.

CHAPTER TWENTY-SIX

Second Chances

The following day, Domina led Hikari, Cole, Macario, and Pal on their quest to Rainbow Falls. As they walked out of the decimated village, the crowds of Fair Folk cleared a path for them. On the sidelines, Pal noticed an elf dressed in black turning his finger and thumb at his lips. The sign of the Locksmiths. Pal never realized their organization transcended planes.

Days passed as the heroes made their way across Elfwood. Domina was invaluable to the party. Her knowledge of the terrain was greater than the elven queen claimed. She tracked the dragon not only by the wreckage he left in his retreat, but also by her acute sense of smell. She could perceive the faintest difference in the air where the dragon flew. And with her keen eyesight, no unturned leaf escaped her.

The party was more than impressed by her, and it was an unspoken truth she ascended to be the new leader. Hikari deferred to her decisions. Macario incessantly questioned her about Elfwood, taking extensive notes on the plane. Pal studied her, but in a less scholarly fashion. He became an expert on the subjects of her legs and back. Her braided hair was a topic for which he desired a hands-on lesson. Hikari sensed Pal's attraction to the elf and smiled to himself. It was the rogue's first open weakness, which made him more trustworthy.

Still bitter from his treatment by the elves, Cole found it difficult to like Domina. But he did respect her. He'd heard bards in taverns sing of rangers; they were scouts and expert trackers who operated best when lost in nature and they were right. Cole admired Domina's knowledge of the Elfwood. He wondered how she could ever inherit the throne when it was so obvious she belonged in the wild.

There were stories of rangers who had the power to communicate with beasts. Domina proved this to be true when she conversed with an osprey. She whistled a perfect imitation of its song.

"We are not far," Domina assured them.

Cole whistled—he couldn't help but imitate Domina—and in a one in a million shot, a hawk swooped down and landed on his outstretched arm.

"Oh my gods, look you guys!"

Domina was not impressed. In fact, she was furious. "Cole! What have you done?"

"Don't be jealous. Who knows? I might be twice the ranger you are."

"Fool. You do not know what you said."

More and more woodland creatures rushed into the clearing. Squirrels, foxes, birds, and mice all scurried toward Cole. His heart pounded with joy.

"Whatever I said must have been pretty great. Check me out. I'm a natural."

When a bear charged out of the bushes, Cole and the others ran away screaming from the roaring grizzly. He made no more attempts to speak with any animals.

The next few hours they climbed glittering pastel hills, crossed great meadows of fluorescent heather, and finally arrived at a roaring turquoise river.

Domina addressed the party. "We head North-South until we reach Rainbow Falls."

"North-South?" Pal asked.

"Are you questioning my leadership?" the princess asked.

"No, I'm questioning your sanity."

"Remember, the realm of Elfwood is not like our own," Macario said and showed Pal the map of Elfwood. The unique compass's directions pointed to North-South, East-West, South-North, and West-East.

"We will camp here for the night," Hikari said. "We can replenish our water supply and get some much-needed rest."

"I'm going to take a bath," Pal said.

"A bath?" Cole asked.

"You know. Wash. You could use one yourself. You reek." Pal said and headed off to the river.

"Do I stink?" Cole asked his wizard friend.

Macario smelled him and said, "Like a troll."

Feeling clean and refreshed from the cold rushing water, Pal climbed out of the river. As naked as the day he was born, he made his way to his clothes draped over a cluster of bushes.

"Interesting tattoo you have," Domina said, appearing on the bank.

He looked at the eye and keyhole inked over his left pectoral, and then at her. "Is that all you're interested in?" Pal asked.

"Your arrogance astounds me. I came to make sure you hadn't run away."

"From you? Never."

Domina shifted her weight to another hip and said, "I know the others trust you, but I don't."

"Hikari doesn't trust me."

"And why is that?"

Pal crossed over to Domina, backed her into the bushes, and said, "Because I'm unpredictable."

Domina caught her breath. "You're incorrigible," she said.

"You're staring."

Tongue tied, Domina grabbed Pal's shirt from behind her and threw it in his face. "Get back to camp as soon as you're dressed. I wouldn't want to lose you to the woods," she said and stormed off.

Pal smiled as he threw his shirt over his head and stepped into his pants.

Gloved hands covered his mouth and pulled him into the bushes. He found himself in a circle of seven Locksmiths. Sarik, Rhonda, Markos, Falor, Pete-Pete, Fellit, the elven thief from the village, and a bearded gnome named Rukis. They were all dressed in the black uniform of their organization.

"Hello, Sarik."

"Why is it I get the strange feeling I can't trust you?"

"I left a trail for you to follow. What more do you want from me?"

"You've made new friends. You wouldn't be planning to betray your family again, would you?"

Pal sighed, threw his hands up in the air, and said, "I give up. I'm undercover and I'm playing my part so well you don't even believe I'm on your side anymore. If I don't play up the hero role, the party won't trust me. If I do, you don't. You're putting me in a no-win situation."

Sarik grinned, revealing a few gold teeth, and said, "Had to ask. Wouldn't be in charge if I didn't cover all my bases, now would I?"

"Can I go now?" Pal asked. "That annoying elf has been up my butt since day one. She'll suspect something if I don't return soon."

Sarik nodded approval and said, "But, you will kill them, won't you?"

"What?"

"After they earn our reward. Once they've done that, they're of no use to us. So you'll kill them, right?"

"I only kill when I have to."

"What kind of an answer is that?" Rukis asked.

"I say we kill them now," Rhonda said, and Markos, Falor, and Pete-Pete agreed.

Rukis drew a curved dagger from his boot and crept over to Pal.

"Sarik, wait!" Pal shouted. "I can get you more than a measly reward."

"I'm listening."

"The princess was taken by a green dragon. We're headed to its lair where there's sure to be more treasure than you could carry."

"I can carry a lot."

"Come on, Sarik," Pal said, "I'm not talking about some lousy reward. I'm talking about a dragon's horde. Diamonds, rubies, sapphires, you name it and it will all be yours."

As Sarik pondered this new plan, Fellit said, "If Il i'Tir lives under the Rainbow Falls, I could lead us there. We don't need him."

The other thieves, especially Rhonda, agreed with the elf.

"No," Sarik said. "Let Pal and his friends go first. They can be our buffer."

"So we have a deal?" Pal asked and extended his hand.

Sarik spat in his own hand, shook Pal's, and said, "Don't forget whose side you're on."

CHAPTER TWENTY-SEVEN

Premonitions

That night at camp, Domina took guard, high in a tree, sharpening her sword on a sandstone. Macario studied his magical tomes and practiced cantrips with his new staff. Hikari warmed himself by the fire. He watched Cole train with an elven polearm Pal "borrowed" for him before they left Elfwick. Cole named the weapon Mud'hir's Claw.

"No, Cole," Hikari said. "The Tongue of Flame combination is parry, parry, slash thrust. Not thrust slash."

Cole roared and threw down Mud'hir's Claw. Domina threw a judgmental glance over her shoulder, and thought, *Hotheaded human. He'll get us all killed.*

"What's wrong?" Hikari asked.

"When Il i'Tir gave me those powers," Cole said. "I was so strong. Without them, I feel so weak."

"Those powers were unnatural," Hikari said. "You're better off without them. In time, your body will readjust."

"We don't have time."

"Patience, Cole."

"Patients are for healers!"

Hikari chuckled, picked up Mud'hir's Claw, handed her to Cole, and said, "Let me tell you a story my cleric Bateren once told me.

"Long, long ago, in the time of darkness, the first child of the world sang. The sun heard her beautiful song from the other side of the world and chased her melody, circled Earth, and turned night into day.

"But when the sun found the first child of the world, she was not singing. She was hard at work, tilling the earth, planting vegetables, and looking after her animals.

"The sun frowned and said, 'Child. Why is it you sing at night and not during the day? Could it be you love the moon more than me?'

"The first child of the world shook her head and said, 'No. I sing at night because it's dark and I am afraid of the dark, and when I am afraid, I sing until I'm not as afraid anymore.'

"The sun thought about this, smiled, and said, 'If you teach me your beautiful song, I will show you the light.'

"The first child of the world agreed to the deal and gave him her song, and he told her his secrets of Starfire."

Hikari ended his story gazing into Cole's eyes with we-just-had-a-moment-look. "What does that have to do with anything?" Cole asked.

Hikari rested a hand on Cole's shoulder. "Although it is the sun who lights our path, it is the children of the world who sing his songs. The true power is within. Follow the light and you will *see*."

Cole shook his head and thought, *having superhuman strength is way more useful than a song.* He sighed, gripped Mud'hir's Claw and resolved to work twice as hard at training. He closed his eyes and dreamed of the power that once pulsed through his body and blood. He had tasted true power and determined to work as hard as he needed to get strong.

Hikari drew the Sun Sword. "You are ready for a more advanced lesson. Stand beside me. Good. Now do exactly as I do."

Cole took his stance next to Hikari and mirrored him, attacking from high and low. Once he got a hang of the sequence, Hikari said, "Again," but defended when Cole attacked and attacked when Cole defended. Together they were impenetrable.

When the exercise came to an end, Hikari and Cole bowed to each other.

"That was amazing!" Cole shouted.

"It has been a long time since I have used the Sun and Shadow technique," Hikari said with a heavy heart. "When we work together, we become one."

"I like it. I can't wait to use it in battle."

"That's enough for tonight." Hikari patted Cole on the arm and sat near the fire.

Pal returned from his bath and whispered in Domina's ear as he passed. "Miss me?"

Her cheeks bloomed roses and she glared at him while preparing a comeback.

Macario stood and spoke the arcane rhyme.

"Sylvanus Staff, raise me now,
High as a raven in the clouds."

Macario rocketed into the air and in a split second, they were all armed. Cole's eyes darted, searching the sky above camp. He didn't know what happened, but was ready for anything.

Macario plummeted back to the earth and landed hard. Smoke billowed from the small crater. Burrowed six feet under, Macario groaned, "Ouch."

Cole leaped into the crater and lifted Macario out. His friend's body smoking in his arms, Cole asked, "What happened?"

"The Sylvanus Staff is more powerful than I thought. I think I broke something on the way down." Macario looked at his legs both dangling in the skin, gruesome question marks. "Yes. I definitely broke something."

"Stand back." Domina retrieved the unicorn's horn from her backpack. She touched the tip of it to both of Macario's legs and the bones popped into place.

Cole's eyes brightened. "The unicorn's horn. When the hobgoblin nearly killed me, I touched the horn and it revived me."

"Unicorns are magical creatures." Macario testing his healed legs with a few squats. "Their horns and blood are renowned for their healing properties."

Cole squinted and rubbed his chin. His thinking posture. "That's why those hobgoblins hunted it," he said.

"How did you know it was a unicorn and not a horse?" Domina asked.

"Uh, the long pointy horn kind of gave it away."

Domina grinned at Cole.

"What's so funny?" he asked.

"Only the Fair Folk and virgins can see unicorns," Macario explained.

Everyone laughed at Cole. Domina laughed at him. Macario laughed at him. Pal. Hikari. Everyone. It was awful and Cole's stomach somersaulted. War drums beat in his ears.

"I haven't met the right girl yet," Cole said.

Pal threw an arm around Cole and said, "There's millions of 'right girls' out there."

The rogue's affection and wise words felt like a sobering bucket of water dousing the fire within Cole. As they walked out of camp, Cole tried to ignore the others' laughter.

"Hey, Pal?"

"Yeah, Cole?"

"Next time, could you not laugh at me? I hate it when people laugh at me. It hurts my feelings, and it makes me want to bash their brains into mush."

Pal shook his head. Cole was genuine and sincere, qualities lacking in most of his previous associations. Sure, he was a bit extreme, but he meant well. Pal slapped him on the shoulder and said, "You got it."

Cole sniffed and wiped his drippy nose. "Thanks, Pal. You're a real friend." Cole headed back to camp shielding his tears. He always got a little teary when it came to best friend stuff. He was new at this.

Pal was too. He had never known someone he could trust before. But he knew he could trust Cole. If Pal had to kill the others to save his own life, so be it. But Cole... How could he save him?

After the party was asleep, a thick black mist rolled into camp. It split into five nightmarish wraiths. These incorporeal goblins bore claws and teeth of smoke and reeked of sulfur. In their presence, plants curled and died, trees wilted, and the grass darkened. The deleterious apparitions stalked forward, relishing the moment before the ambush.

The wraiths barked orders at each other, clouds of hate, divvying up their victims. Their foul speech woke Domina from her dream, and she wasted no time leaping into action. She grabbed a flaming log from the fire and plunged the torch into one of the creeping wraiths. It disappeared, howling in pain. Domina tumbled around the fire and kicked another flaming log into her free hand. To her surprise, the wraiths whirled into thin snakes of mist and flew into the sleeping heroes' noses.

Cole's dream shifted into realms of fear and humiliation. Pal's slumber was disturbed by overwhelming guilt and loneliness. Macario's nightmare filled with rejection and feelings of inadequacy. Hikari suffered more than the rest.

Deep within the caverns of Heaven's Peak, the tallest mountain in the kingdom, the paladin ran from a twenty-foot tall white dragon coated in wooly feathers. The wyvern licked the paladin's blood from her white beak and sucked his flesh from her dark talons.

Four deep claw marks ripped into the paladin's cheek. He stumbled into a dark cave, fumbling at the walls. He did not check to see how much distance he put between himself and the beast. Dragging a black katana, he left a shadowy trail in the snow covered ground.

The paladin stopped. The unmistakable smell of vinegar wafted from the darkness. There were two dragons. Trapped and too weak to fight, the paladin raised his dark sword above him and cast a shadow over himself. And not a second too late.

Sniffing the air for his prey, the male dragon stalked by. Though the paladin's scent was fresh, he went unseen. The female dragon waited for her mate to find their meal.

The paladin watched the wyverns hunt from the safety of his shadow. After the longest minute of his life, the female grew impatient and left in search of a quicker meal. The male followed, but breathed a gust of ice and snow into the shadows behind him, trapping the paladin within a block of ice.

Sweating profusely, Hikari tossed and turned in his bedroll.

Cole shook him and said, "Wake up, Hikari!"

Domina ordered Cole to stand back, lowered her torch, and burned Hikari's chest. He woke shrieking and exhaled a misty wraith. In a flash, Hikari drew the Sun Sword and thrust it into the wraith, which glowed with sunlight and burst.

"Hikari, are you alright?" Cole asked.

"Yes," the paladin said. "I had a nightmare vision."

"We all did," Cole said. "Domina saved us."

"Thank you," Pal said.

"You would have done the same for me," the elven princess replied without making eye contact.

"What were those things?" Cole asked.

"Wraiths," Macario said. "Aspects of goblins. Carriers of dark premonitions and nightmares. We're not safe here."

Domina corrected him, "We are not safe anywhere."

CHAPTER TWENTY-EIGHT

Rainbow Falls

The party covered stretches of land scourged by the wraiths. Domina worried what befell Elfwick. She doubted her mother's decision to send her on this impetuous adventure. She should be with the other rangers, defending their home. What benefit would the elves gain from saving a long forgotten princess? Their race's ties with humans were too strained for repair. She doubted any good would come from restored relations. Certainly, the humans would benefit, but the elves? Not likely.

The party came to a great waterfall crashing onto rapids below. A perpetual rainbow arced over a whirlpool.

Domina pointed. "The dragon's lair must be hidden in the cave through these falls," she said.

"Can you levitate us across?" Cole asked Macario.

"I can only levitate objects up and down. It would take a flying spell to cover any ground."

"Okay. Then fly us across."

"I don't know that spell," Macario confessed.

"What good is a wizard who can't fly?" Pal asked.

"I apologize if I am not all powerful. Perhaps you would like to memorize an ancient language, practice the corresponding hand signals that accompany each spell, and perform both exactly as required?"

"I'm sorry," Pal said.

"There is a reason it is called the Arcane Arts."

"Alright. Alright."

"I may owe you a life debt, but I am not your puppet."

"I said I'm sorry!"

"Both of you stop," Cole pleaded. "This isn't us. We're a team."

"You're right," Macario admitted. "The wraith's effects may have lasted longer than expected. Please accept my apology."

"Don't worry about it," Pal said and shook his hand.

Domina nocked her bow with a grappling arrow. "Now that you boys have finished squabbling, shall we continue?"

She shot the grappling arrow through the waterfall. The arrow planted in hard rock hidden behind the falls and she handed the rope to Hikari.

"Why can't I go first?" Cole whined.

Domina sighed and handed the rope to Cole, who took it and swung across the whirlpool into the hidden cave. Domina nocked three more grappling arrows and fired them across the rushing water. Hikari and Macario swung to the other side.

Domina held the third rope out for Pal.

"I can do it myself," he said, tied a rope to one of his daggers, aimed, and threw it over the whirlpool. When it wrapped around a jutting rock, he swung across.

Domina snorted. "Humans," she said and followed Pal through the falls and landed with grace in pitch black.

Hikari drew the Sun Sword and illuminated the moldy cave. Mud and puddles covered the floor. Tiny pink fairies with bat wings hung upside down from white hairy roots in the ceiling.

"Pixies!" Macario exclaimed.

"Mischievous tricksters," Domina warned. "Best to ignore them."

As the heroes walked deeper into the cave, Cole was drawn to the pixies, charmed by their beauty. One pixie hanging by her clawed toes to a ceiling root teetered back and forth. Without opening her mouth, she said to Cole telepathically, *Aren't I beautiful? Don't you want to touch me? I can be yours forever.*

Cole let the others pass and plucked the pixie from the root. She waltzed in his palm and enchanted him with her grace.

Pal glanced over his shoulder and saw Cole lagging behind. "What are you doing?" he asked.

"Cole! Don't!" Domina shouted, a second too late.

Cole tried to pet the pixie with his index finger, but she threw a flash of sparkling light into his eyes. His vision went black and Cole dropped her into a puddle. The pixie rolled and splashed, giggling with delight. Blind, Cole staggered in circles, cursing at the wretched little thing. He accidentally stepped on the giggling pixie. The cavern of sleeping pixies opened their eyes, red and glowing with ferocity.

"Run!" Domina shouted.

Pal grabbed Cole's hand and led him deeper into the cave.

"I can't see!" Cole shouted.

Pal looked over his shoulder and saw hundreds of pixies swarming toward them. "Trust me," he said, "you don't want to see!"

The furious pixies sprayed sparkling bolts of energy at the fleeing heroes.

Domina yelled at Cole, "Oaf! Next time, keep your hands to yourself!"

"Stop picking on him," Pal said.

"I'm trying to keep us alive and this oaf is going to get us killed."

"What does *oaf* mean?" Cole asked.

"A stupid, uncultured, and clumsy person," Macario said matter-of-factly.

"Hey!"

"Quiet. All of you," Hikari said.

The pixies chased them deeper into the cave. The Sun Sword lit their path, but Domina's keen elf eyes saw their escape route first.

"Look. There in the distance." Domina pointed to an ancient gate embedded in the rock, *The Void* written in iron above the arch.

"Pal, I need you to pick the lock," Hikari said.

"Got it," he said reaching for his tools.

"Cole, stay behind Domina. Macario, we need a distraction to give Pal enough time."

"Let me think of something."

"Make it quick," Hikari said as they came to the wall.

The pixies closed in on them, ready to unleash their wrath. An idea came to him and Macario snapped his fingers. He grabbed his water skin and filled his mouth. He made a circle with his index finger and thumb and blew magical bubbles at the pixies. Delighted, they forgot to avenge their squished sister. They flew about giggling and popping the bubbles.

Pal succeeded in picking the gate's lock. He led everyone though the gate and into The Void, but he did not lock the gate behind him.

The Void was a dark and empty plane before Il i'Tir built his lair. Neither cold nor warm, the air was still and all was quiet. Using dark magic, he threw fire diamonds into the ether to light his domain. He brought a disk of earth from Elfwood and paved it with flagstones. He planted towering walls of weeds and thorns to ward off intruders. Over the years, animals, birds, and insects followed the dragon into The Void and populated it with life.

The party stood in a courtyard looking at an opening in the wall. There were blood stains and skeletons strewed across the yard. It was impossible to tell if they died running to, or from, the entrance.

"Where are we now?" Cole asked.

"Outside of a labyrinth," Macario said.

The bramble tower loomed a mile away at the center of the maze.

"Mud'hir Erta!" Domina cried.

"The tower's architecture is sylvan," Macario said.

Hikari stroked his mustache. "Since when do the sylvans form alliances with dragons?"

"It's certainly unprecedented," Macario said.

Domina balled her hand into a fist. "How could they betray our people like this?"

"Who knows what Il i'Tir holds over them," Pal said.

"I'd rather die than betray my own race," Domina said.

"Gosh!" Cole exclaimed. "I wish I could see what you guys see. Everything sounds so awesome and deadly!"

"Stay close," Hikari said. "We don't know what evils lurk inside these briar walls."

The party drew their weapons and entered the labyrinth.

CHAPTER TWENTY-NINE

Through the Labyrinth

C ole held onto Domina's shoulder. He followed her through thousands of twists and turns in the labyrinth. Without sight, his other senses amplified. Crickets trumpeted, toads bellowed, and birds wailed. The labyrinth smelled of holly and poinsettia, ivy and mistletoe, rosewood and spruce. It was an odd dichotomy of sweet scents and alarming sounds. Each step he took unsettled him. Slipping on the occasional stray rock, or tripping over an upended root, made his heart race. Domina assured him the pixie's spell would not last forever.

Pal brooded over her insistence that she lead Cole when he could take his friend's hand. Domina wanted to keep watch over Cole, to avoid any other accidents that may result in their deaths. She wanted to be free of him as much as he did not want to rely on her. Still, Pal was jealous.

For hours, they navigated the maze. Hikari led the party, the Sun Sword in hand, ready to smite any foes. Macario followed behind, scribbling a rough map of the labyrinth. Pal kept to the rear, shaving thorns from the briar walls.

"What are you doing?" Domina asked.

"Leaving a trail in case we ever want to get out of here. What do you think I'm up to?"

Before she could reply, Hikari shouted, "Quiet! I've had enough of your bickering."

"Yeah," Cole chimed in, "we're a team. We need to stick together if we're going to survive."

The party walked in silence. Twists and turns led them to another dead end. Hikari rubbed his temple and scanned the twisting walls for their next route.

"Are we there yet?" Cole asked him.

"No."

"Why did we stop?"

Hikari remained silent.

"Are we lost?"

"For Rey's sake, Cole! Give me a minute to think."

Macario placed a calming hand on Hikari's shoulder and said, "Let's retrace our steps."

The party turned and followed Pal's trail of thorns until a wall blocked their path.

"What the...?!" Pal exclaimed.

"The walls keep shifting," Hikari said and seethed.

"Well, the good news is, I can sort of see again," Cole said.

Hikari roared with frustration and began hacking at the briar with his glowing sword. Embers flurried through the narrow passage. One caught Domina's shoulder and left a pinpoint burn.

"Hikari, calm down!" she shouted.

The paladin stopped and panted, his hair stuck to his forehead with sweat. Cole noticed he had been on edge ever since the wraith attack.

"Forgive me," Hikari said. "I lost myself for a moment."

"If you ask me, you had a pretty good idea," Cole said and hacked away at the wall with his Mud'hir's Claw, making a tunnel. "Sometimes you have to cheat if you want to win."

Pal wagged a finger at Cole and said, "He's learning."

For about five minutes, Cole hacked a narrow path through the wall and the others followed behind.

"Anyone wanna help?" Cole griped.

"We are too close together," Hikari said.

Cole huffed and cut down another large chunk of the wall. Something underfoot quaked and the walls of the maze swayed and moaned.

"What was that?" Cole asked.

"The walls are alive," Macario said. "Death is imminent. How exciting."

Cole hacked faster and faster through the briar. The walls started to pinch Pal and Domina behind him. They shouted for Cole to cut faster.

"I'm going as fast as I can!" he shouted, and hacked away at the last bit of wall until a clearing revealed itself on the other side. Cole, Hikari, and Macario ran out through the opening. Pal shoved Domina ahead to safety. He threw himself after her, drawing his legs close to his body as the walls closed and the tunnel disappeared.

Pal landed on top of Domina and quickly rolled off her. No thanks spoken, they shared an awkward glance that said enough.

The heroes found themselves standing in an exotic garden. A rainbow of pods, flowers, mushrooms, and bushes surrounded a fruit tree ripe with plums, apples, lemons, oranges, bananas, and berries.

Cole clapped his hands together and said, "Thank the gods! I'm starving!" But when he reached for a pear, Domina caught his wrist and shook her head.

"If you're hungry," she held up a loaf of elven bread.

Cole stuck out his tongue. "No thanks," he said. "I've eaten enough elven bread for a lifetime."

The party ate slices of elven bread, drank from their water skins, and rested as Cole explored the garden. A bed of polka-dot mushrooms grew at the base of the fruit tree. Cole licked his lips and glanced over his shoulder.

Domina wasn't looking.

Cole smiled and plucked one of the mushrooms, double checked to see if Domina noticed. She had not, and he devoured the moist flavorful mushroom in one bite and picked the rest of them. He ate half, and stored the rest in his pack.

"Missed one," he said and plucked the stray mushroom. Examining it, he wondered, *how could something so strange looking be so delicious?* Indeed, the mushroom looked strange. It changed colors, fuchsia to auburn to lime to bronze, on and on it went. In fact, the entire garden became a light show of splendid colors. Cole stumbled around the garden enjoying the spectacle.

Domina rolled her eyes and asked, "What has he done now?"

"Cole? Are you alright?" Hikari asked, concerned.

"Pretty," Cole said. He waddled toward a large clump of fuchsia pods with the balance and coordination of a toddler. He stroked the small wiry hairs covering one of the bigger pods and it opened. A pink stigma flopped out like a tongue.

"Nice doggie," Cole said, reaching for the stigma.

"Cole, don't!" Pal cried.

The pod snapped closed, missing Cole's hand.

"No biting!" he scolded and reached out again.

An arrow flew through the air and pinned the pod's mouth shut.

Domina lowered her bow and shouted, "Get away from there, Cole!"

The pod writhed in pain and the other pods followed suit, wriggling like the tentacles of a kraken. A low hum like the moaning walls spread through the garden.

Pal, Hikari, and Macario dropped their bread and drew their weapons. The entire world tilted and Cole found it difficult to keep his balance. Vines shot out of the walls and snared them one by one. They were lifted into the air and brought before the fruit tree. Its bark cracked and split, and a ten-foot tall woman of wood stepped out of the tree trunk. The dryad was a sentinel of nature. She had arms and legs of branches, fingers and toes of twigs, her hair of moss, and eyes of acorns.

"You dare harm my precious garden?" the dryad asked. "An elf should know better."

"I am Domina, princess of Elfwood. Release us, dryad, and all will be forgiven."

"Those who harm my garden face my wrath," the dryad said and called upon buried roots to surface. They formed a cage and the vines dropped them in except for Cole. The vine tightened around his waist and brought him over to the dryad so she could look him in the eyes.

"Wee!" Cole sang, enjoying the ride.

"You shall be punished first," the dryad said.

Cole poked her nose. "Boop."

Macario recited a memorized spell,

"Lengthen ears, whiskers and feet,

Fur and tail makes my spell complete."

He tapped Pal's legs with his staff. Pal transformed into a cottontail rabbit. He hopped out of the cage, rubbed his nose, groomed his whiskers, and chewed through the cage's grassy lock.

Hikari charged out, brandishing flaming steel, and slashed at the dryad. In a blink, she transformed herself to stone. The Sun Sword careened off her rocky surface. The dryad transformed back to her wooden form and spit thorns from her mouth like a rapid fire blowpipe. Many thorns found their way through Hikari's chainmail armor and he fell.

Cole dangled in the air. The violent turn of events had sobered him up. He reached for his fallen friend and mentor. "Hikari!"

Cole tugged at the vine wrapped around his torso, but couldn't break free, and had to watch the battle he desired to join.

Hidden in the cage for protection, Macario opened one of his magical tomes. He frantically searched for a spell. Cute, but distracting, Pal hopped around his feet.

"I'll change you back. I just need a minute to find the right spell."

Domina nocked her bow with three arrows and shot the dryad, who reeled in pain and turned to mud, disappearing into the earth.

"Nice shot," Hikari said. He pushed himself to his feet with a groan and pulled a bloody thorn from his side, dropping it.

Vines sprouted from the ground under Domina's feet and wove up her legs, immobilizing her.

"Hikari!" she shouted.

The paladin moved forward, readying his sword.

The dryad burst out of the ground in front of Domina and slammed her arm into Hikari. Landing hard on his back, the thorns dug deeper into his flesh.

The dryad faced the elf. Her acorn eyes dim, she tightened the vines gripping Domina. The elven princess unleashed a cry of pain most unbecoming, not of her royal stature, but of her military standing. Pal the cottontail rabbit bounded to her rescue. He chewed the vines away with his enlarged teeth.

In the cage, Macario found the spell he sought, recited the arcane rhyme,

"Crack the ground beneath my foe
Mighty now, a thousand foot throw."

He slammed his staff on the ground. A fissure rippled from the staff to the ground beneath the dryad. The grass underfoot trembled and solidified into a plank. The dryad looked at Macario, who waved goodbye to her. She catapulted out of the garden, over the labyrinth walls, and out of sight.

They heard a distant *pffft* and the life in the garden vanished. The vines released Cole and he plummeted to the ground. A second later, he was back on his feet as if nothing had happened.

"Whoa!" he exclaimed. "That was incredible!"

Hikari cut Domina free. Macario picked the rabbit up by its ears and tapped it on the head with his staff, returning Pal to human form.

"Macario?"

"Yes, Pal?"

"I know that worked, but next time you want to change me into a rabbit, ask first."

"I promise."

Cole stumbled forward with a goofy smile. "You guys have to try these mushrooms."

Domina kicked herself free from the last of the vines. "Imbecile! You're always causing trouble and I've had enough. If we are to continue on this quest, Cole stays behind."

All the joy drained from Cole. "That's not fair!"

"What's not fair is you constantly endangering the lives of the entire group. I call for a vote. All in favor of leaving Cole behind until we find the princess, raise your hand," Domina said and threw her hand up.

Cole gasped when Hikari raised his hand. "Hikari?!"

"You may not be ready for this mission," he said. "It would be best if you stayed behind and practiced your drills."

Cole felt as if he would faint.

"What about you, Macario?" Domina asked. "How do you vote?"

"Cole should stay with us."

"Thank you!"

"He may die if we leave him on his own," Macario added.

"He'll be fine," Domina said.

"Don't I get to vote?" Cole asked.

"You are a member of this party," Hikari said. "So, yes."

"Good," Cole said. "I vote I don't get left behind. There. It's settled. Can we keep moving now?"

"Wait," Domina said. "Pal hasn't voted."

Pal had not voted, because he had been watching the situation unfold. He scratched his stubbly chin, biding his time, thinking of his answer. But there was only one answer. He knew it would break Cole's heart, but he wouldn't let his best friend die at the hands of the Locksmiths.

"Sorry, Cole," Pal said and raised his hand.

Cole choked back a tear. His eyes hot and chin quivering, he said, "But, I'm the glue."

Pal's stomach churned. "You can protect the camp," he said.

Cole turned his back to Pal because he didn't want him to see him cry. It would have only proved Domina right. He wasn't ready to be a hero.

Cole sat at the base of the fruit tree with his back to the party. Goodbyes were not exchanged when they split up.

CHAPTER THIRTY

Maisie

Hikari, Domina, Macario, and Pal navigated the treacherous maze in silence. Infinite twists and turns led them to dead end after dead end. Without Cole, the party was able to focus and work without stress.

Cole sat in the dryad's garden, battling the demons in his head. They told him, *you're not good enough* and *your dreams will never come true* and *you should have given up long ago*. These thoughts crashed down on him, heavy as an ocean wave, drowning him in his own sorrow.

Cole slammed the back of his head against the mixed fruit tree to quash the voices. Oranges, bananas, and peaches shook on the branches above. Over and over again, Cole punished himself against the trunk of the tree.

An lemon fell from its branch and landed on his head. It rolled off his dome and landed at his side. Cole stared at the stupid lemon. He hated it. He hated everything right now. He picked up the lemon and flung it in the bushes. It hit something that squeaked. A moment later, a tiny black rat crawled out of the bushes and into the garden. It stood upright, sniffing the air, and rubbed its pink paws together. The rat stared at Cole as if waiting for something.

"What do you want?" Cole asked.

"Aren't you going to apologize?" the rat replied.

Cole wondered if the poisonous mushrooms were still playing tricks with his mind. "Am I imagining this, or are you a talking rat?" he asked.

"I'm real all right. Yep, yep."

"I'm sorry..."

"The name is Maisie. You've made it farther through the labyrinth than anyone has before."

"No, I haven't. There are four other heroes further through it than me. I was slowing them down."

"If you ask me, you all look a little lost," Maisie said. "Where are you going anyways?"

"We're trying to make it to the bramble tower."

"Why in heaven's name would you want to go there?" Maisie asked, appalled at the thought.

"We're going to save the princess."

"Princess Oriel?"

"That's her."

"What's the use in saving that old hag? You're a nice strapping boy. You should be rescuing girls your own age," Maisie said, her whiskers curled in a smile. "You should see her daughter." Maisie whistled. "Fine looking girl for a half-dragon."

"Tara?"

"Yep, yep. She's got a temper. I've seen what she does to goblins who disobey her. Yikes. I wouldn't want to cross her. No siree!"

"Ugh!" Cole exclaimed and kicked up a heap of dirt that landed an inch from Maisie. "This sucks! A dragon-warlock, a half-dragon princess, and a gazillion goblins. It's what I dreamed of as a kid, Maisie. At the orphanage, all the other kids dreamed of mommies and daddies to come take them away. But I dreamed of adventure. Fighting trolls, slaying giants, riding dolphins, you know, hero stuff. Now I'm here, so close to fame and glory I can taste it, and I'm not even going to get a chance to help."

"Why not?" Maisie asked.

"Because the party voted me out of the group."

"Vote? That doesn't sound fair at all," Maisie said. "We rats let the most powerful in the colony calls the shots. Now that makes sense. Yep, yep." Maisie rubbed her nose. "Anyway, all you groups trying to get in the bramble tower are out of your minds. Yep, yep"

"What do you mean, *all you groups*?"

Maisie groomed herself. "Well, there's your group of friends and the other group of scary thieves."

Cole almost jumped out of his boots. "Thieves?" he asked. "What did they look like?"

"Well, they were all scary. The leader was bald as an egg. Had himself a black dagger. Played with it between his fingers, he did. Yep, yep."

Cole rubbed his chin like Hikari when he contemplated. "Whoever these scary guys are, I have to warn the others," he said. "I'm the glue for goodness sake. We're supposed to stick together!" This new sense of importance inspired Cole. "You seem to know a lot about the area, Maisie. Will you please join me on my quest as a guide?"

Maisie tapped her chin with a tiny pink finger. "What's in it for me?"

"You can have my elven bread."

Maisie smiled a large bucktooth grin and said, "Now we're talking. Yep, yep."

CHAPTER THIRTY-ONE

The Bramble Tower

Cole fed Maisie a slice of elven bread. As the tiny rat pigged out, she taught Cole the labyrinth's three rules.

"First rule, never turn around," she said with a full mouth, crumbs falling onto her hairy chest and belly. "This labyrinth doesn't play fair. Nope, nope. The second you walk backward, all roads lead to the beginning and you have to start all over again.

"Second rule, look but don't touch. That nasty dryad, she senses anything that happens in her garden. You pick one flower, step on one twig, or look funny at a tree, she'll get you. Yep, yep."

"What's the third rule?" Cole asked.

"Always have enough bread to keep your guide happy."

Cole smiled and gave Maisie another slice of elven bread. "So where do we go from here?" he asked.

Maisie sucked her fingers clean. "I say the best way to go through the labyrinth, is to go under it."

Maisie rolled onto all fours and scurried into the bushes. Cole followed and found the rat with her hands on her hips, standing in front of a manhole.

"Help me lift this thing will you?" she asked.

Hikari, Domina, Macario, and Pal found their way to the center of the labyrinth. There was a large stretch of farmland between them, and the tower loomed in the distance. The heroes hesitated to step out into the open. Who knew what lay beyond the safety of the labyrinth?

"What's that foul smell?" Domina asked.

"Goblin babies," Macario said. He pointed to row after row of what looked like a cabbage-patch if the cabbage were turds. "Goblins are grown in mud. Nice and warm and sloppy."

"There must be a thousand," Pal said.

"More like a hundred thousand," Macario said.

"They're breeding an army," Hikari said.

A team of goblin harvesters walked through the fields. Where an ox would usually be, was a hobgoblin pulling a plow. Domina drew her bow and nocked an arrow.

"Hold on," Hikari said. "The bramble tower is ahead."

"I have a clear shot."

"Better not to draw unnecessary attention. Macario?"

The wizard waved his staff at the goblin harvesters and spoke arcane rhyme,

"Goblin tooth, warts, and stare
Make us mirror the goblins there,"

He tapped his the staff on each them and transformed the party into goblins.

Goblin Pal frowned at goblin Macario and said, "What did I say about changing me?"

"You said the next time I change you into a rabbit, I should ask you first," goblin Macario replied. "Does that also go for me changing you into a goblin?"

"Stop changing me!"

"I think it's an improvement," goblin Domina said.

"Hush," goblin Hikari said. "We need to blend in."

The goblin harvesters tilled the fertile earth and planted goblin seeds, which aren't actually seeds, but body parts of dead goblins. And after a three week gestation period, the planted eyeballs, toenails, fingers, noses, ears, and snouts blossom into hideous goblins. Only the heart of a goblin would grow into a hobgoblin, limiting their production.

Disguised as goblins, the heroes passed without conflict, but not without suspicious stares. The other goblins wondered why they dressed in human and elf clothes and pinched their noses. One goblin harvester took a deep whiff of the ogre dung fertilizer and thought, *Ahh! That's the good stuff!*

Once the party crossed the goblin breeding grounds, they came to another obstacle. Two sylvan guards, armed with heavy shields and longswords, flanked the doors into the bramble tower. Their blond hair was drawn back into ponytails underneath their helmets. The goblin-heroes approached and the sylvan guards slammed their swords against their shields.

"Halt, pests!" a guard ordered. "No one enters without lord Il i'Tir's permission."

"Lord," goblin Domina repeated with distaste and rolled her eyes.

"We are here to relieve you," goblin Pal said.

The second guard narrowed his eyes and said, "Our shift just started."

Goblin Macario leaned on his staff and said, "And I'm sure you guys are exhausted. We'll take over from here." The goblin wizard smiled a hideous goblin smile, full of filthy yellowed teeth.

The guards looked at each other. Something strange was up. They raised their swords.

"Guess that didn't work," goblin Pal said.

Macario released his goblin disguise spell. The party returned to their natural forms. The sylvan guards stumbled back and bumped into the doors.

"Two against four," Pal said. "The odds are against you."

Seven more sylvan soldiers ran up from behind. Nine against four. The sylvan guards at the door smiled sinisterly.

"You know what," Pal said, "you guys seem to have it covered here. We'll be leaving now."

The reinforcements surrounded the party and confiscated their weapons. Hikari handed over the Sun Sword and said, "A paladin's sword is of no use to you."

One of the soldiers spoke with a voice coarser than gravel. "Let's see about that."

He spun around and plunged the Sun Sword into the chest of one of the door guards. The other guard was so shocked, he did not even block the next attack and his head fell from his shoulders.

Pal looked at the two dead guards at his feet and up at their killer who removing his helmet. Pal gasped.

"Sarik?!"

Minutes before, Maisie led Cole through the dark, grungy, and slippery pipes of the labyrinth's massive sewers. They smelled worse than a demon. Cole pinched his nose so hard he was afraid it might pop. After the longest and smelliest twenty minutes of his life, the pair passed a nest of rats.

"Hey, guys!" Maisie said to Cole, "They can't talk back, but talking to them keeps me sane." Maisie hummed a little tune and carried on.

"So how is it you can talk?" Cole asked.

"You never met a talking rat before?"

"Nope."

"Hmm. My mom always said I was special, but I thought she had to say that. Ah. Here we are."

They arrived at the foot of an old but sturdy ladder. Cole lifted Maisie by the scruff of her neck, placed her on his shoulder, and climbed up. Upon breaching the surface, Cole inhaled deep gulps of fresh air that was sweet and made him a little light-headed. Once he caught his breath, he stared at the bramble tower in all its glory. He craned his head back to see the top of the tower.

Cole heard two death cries on the other side of the tower. "Hold on, Maisie."

"To what?" she asked.

Cole dashed around the bramble tower, Mud'hir's Claw held high in the air. Maisie clung to his collar, her eyes bulging with fear at his war cry.

His barbaric scream startled the Locksmiths. Hikari, Domina, Pal, and Macario all knew it was Cole and shook their heads. They all thought, *He didn't listen. Of course, he didn't listen!*

Sarik turned, twirling the Sun Sword in his hands. Cole came into view screaming his psychotic battle cry. Sarik sneered and said to Pal, "Handle this."

Pal swallowed what remained of his honor, ran over to Cole, and asked, "What are you doing here?"

Cole stopped yelling; confused, slowed his charge, and said, "I came to rescue you guys."

Pal snarled, "You should have stayed at the camp."

Cole's heart sunk and he lowered Mud'hir's Claw and joined the party. "I was trying to help. You see, I met this talking rat..."

Maisie waved at them and said, "I'm Maisie. Yep, yep."

Macario waved back.

Cole continued. "Maisie said there were some scary people following you. She knew a secret passage under the labyrinth, so I came to warn you, but you guys seem to have it all under control. I guess what I wanted to say is, I'm sorry. I'm sorry I touch things I shouldn't and I always get us into trouble..."

"Cole...," Pal said.

"Let me finish. I'm sorry I'm always getting us into trouble, but the truth is you guys always get us out of trouble. Without me, there wouldn't be any excitement and if you're not looking for excitement, I don't even know why you would want to be in the hero business to begin with." Cole concluded and exhaled a long satisfying breath. "Phew. I've been waiting to get that off my chest for some time now. So, who are these guys and why do they have our weapons?" he asked.

Sarik said, "We meet again, boy."

"Do I know you?" Cole asked and Sarik slapped him. "Oh, now I remember. You're that jerk from the Drunken Skeleton."

"Alright," Pal said. "I brought you this far, forget about him and let's go get the treasure."

Cole squinted. "What's going on, Pal?"

Domina said with contempt, "Don't you see? Your 'pal' betrayed us."

Cole shot his friend a pleading look. "Pal?"

"I'm sorry, Cole."

Rhonda stepped behind Domina, drew a short sword, and said, "I say we slit their throats now."

"What do you say, Pal?" Sarik asked.

Pal found it hard to swallow. "Let them live until we're sure we don't need them."

All the Locksmiths but Sarik groaned.

"I told you he's a traitor," Rhonda said.

"You want proof I'm not a traitor?"

The Locksmiths answered with a collective, "Yes!"

Pal drew a knife from his boot and plunged it into Cole's chest. The entire party gasped. Cole's eyes flashed open, two swirling blue pools of disbelief. He opened his mouth, but the pain was too great to speak. All he could manage were a few guttural clicks.

"Good luck saving the princess," Pal said, oozing sarcasm.

Cole closed his eyes and fell. Dead.

"Villain!" Hikari bellowed, charging at Pal.

Sarik stepped between them and cut Hikari along his belly with the Sun Sword as he passed, and the paladin fell.

Grabbing his waist, warm blood seeped through Hikari's chainmail into his fingers.

"I thought paladins were tough," Sarik sneered.

Macario kneeled beside Hikari and the two men held each other and cried. Maisie bowed her head, and Domina, shivering with fury, glared at Pal.

"I always knew I could trust you," Sarik said, slapped Pal on the back, and barked orders at two of his men. "Marcus! Falor! Dispose of the bodies and take up a post outside. The rest of you, follow me. There's treasure to be had!"

CHAPTER THIRTY-TWO

New Lows

The Locksmiths and their prisoners descended into the depths of the bramble tower. Glowing fire diamonds fixed on the dangerous thorned walls lit the way. Sarik took point, carrying Maisie in his clenched fist. He promised to let her live if she guided them to the treasury. Playing guide was an easy decision for the talking rat. She would take them to the treasury, wish them luck, and scurry home to the safety of the sewers.

Hikari, Macario, and Domina were despondent. Cole had been the glue. With him dead, the group fell apart. Pal walked behind them holding a short sword to Domina's back, and blocking the only escape route.

"Tell me, Pal," she said. "What did they promise you? Riches? Women? You make me sick."

"I had no choice."

"You always have a choice. And you chose to murder your best friend," Domina said, anger floating above her sinking heart. "I'm a fool. I thought you were my friend too." She shook her head, disgusted. "Hikari was right. You are a villain."

Pal throat closed, but as hard as it was, he did what he knew he had to do and prayed the fates would take care of the rest. He sneaked over to Macario and whispered, "I don't want to hurt any of you. You have to believe me."

Macario squinted and a tear fell down his cheek.

Pal went on, "Don't you know any spells that could help?"

The wizard said, "If I did, I'd make you disappear."

"Shut up, you idiots!" Sarik barked. "We're here!"

Sylvan soldiers patrolled the hallways of the bramble tower's lowest level. Six marched by in single file and two small steel balls rolled into the corridor. They halted and the first in line bent down to inspect them. Gas sprayed into the air, concealing a sneak attack. When the air cleared, there were six dead sylvan soldiers.

Sarik peeked around a corner. He spied a door with draconic runes etched on its face, guarded by ten sylvan soldiers.

"That's the treasury," Maisie said.

"How do you know?" Sarik asked.

"You don't station ten soldiers outside the loo."

"Watch your tongue, rat, or I'll cut it out."

"The name's Maisie and I don't think you're very nice. Nope-nope."

Sarik threw Maisie over his shoulder and she landed hard on the floor in front of Macario. The wizard bent down, picked her up gently, and asked, "Are you hurt?"

"Not as bad as egg head will be when I'm through with him," she said, kicking and scratching the air.

"How do you want to take it?" Rhonda asked Sarik.

"We'll need a distraction."

They looked at the heroes.

One of the sylvan soldiers said "What the...?"

Hikari, Macario, Maisie, and Domina approached.

Maisie waved her tiny pink hand, and called, "Hey there!"

The soldier shouted, "Intruders! Seize them!"

The sylvan soldiers surrounded the heroes. Before they could arrest them, the Locksmiths attacked. A swirl of steel rampaged, and seconds later, the sylvan soldiers were relieved of duty.

Rhonda went right to work on the door. She solved its runic puzzle. Spinning dials and setting hieroglyphs in the correct order, the door unlocked and Sarik pushed past her.

The treasury glowed with precious stones and artifacts. Mounds of gold, silver, and platinum coins from kingdoms of every corner of Eld sparkled. Magnificent weapons glowed with enchantment.

Sarik smiled a toothless grin and said, "Take as much as you can."

The Locksmiths laughed and rushed into the room. They were so greedy to steal as much treasure as possible, they seemed to forget their prisoners.

A shining greatsword caught Domina's eye. And when she thought no one was looking, she inched closer to it.

Rhonda caught her wrist and said, "Try that again and I'll cut your hand off."

Fellit glanced around the room, confused, and asked, "Where's Pal?"

The green dragon Il i'Tir reclined on his mossy throne. He gazed into the Eye of Nero, an orb clutched in his paw. Inside he watched a massive, volcanic red dragon and an army of lizard-men assemble at the base of his mountain fortress, Donto Borba. Tara stood at her father's side, the orb's visions reflected on her polished black Minotaur helmet.

The doors to the throne room opened. A wary goblin harvester entered, escorted by two sylvan soldiers.

"Now what?!" the dragon bellowed.

The goblin was nervous, but determined to relay his important observation. "Pardon me, your grace. But something fishy's going on."

"Get to the point, pest!" Tara shouted. She had no tolerance for goblins.

The goblin cowered before her. "We saw strange looking goblins approaching the tower," it said, averting its eyes.

Tara placed her boot on the goblin's head and pushed it down to the floor. She pressed her full weight down on its skull. "All goblins look strange."

The goblin was in agony. "Yes Princess Tara. But these were especially strange. They wore human clothes!"

"Distractions, distractions," Il i'Tir waved a dismissive claw and returned his focus to the Eye of Nero. "Lieutenant!" Adrias, the sylvan lieutenant stepped forward. "Look into it!"

A baritone voice spoke from a dark corner of the throne room, "Don't bother." Pal stepped out of the shadows and leaned against a timber pillar.

Behind the heavy black Minotaur helmet, Tara's emerald eyes squinted as she sized Pal up. The attractive human dressed in black didn't seem a threat, but he had managed to sneak in undetected. Tara's hand grasped the boomerang blade holstered in her belt.

"I've come to warn you," Pal said, checking his fingernails for grime.

The goblin harvester pointed at him and exclaimed, "That's one of the strange goblins I saw!"

Tara used the goblin's head as a step ladder and squashed it like a melon. Bits of blood and brain splattered on the floor. In an instant, a team of goblin house slaves mopped up the mess.

Pal picked grit from his thumbnail with one of his daggers and blew the dirt from its tip. A good two feet taller, Tara towered over him. "You have guts, little man," she said looking down at the rogue. "Let's hear what he has to say, father."

Il i'Tir used a hind leg to scratch an itch behind his frilled skull plate. "If we must," he said, his attention still fixed on the orb's visions of the crimson dragon, Hexor.

Pal kept his casual attitude and leaned against the pillar. He asked, "Don't you remember me?"

Il i'Tir took a deep breath through his nostrils, turned his attention away from the Eye of Nero. "All humans look alike to a dragon."

"I bet you'd be able to tell Cole from a group of humans," Pal said.

Il i'Tir narrowed his yellow eyes. "Cole?" he asked.

"Yeah. Your cellmate in the elven dungeons. The dumb kid on a quest to rescue the princess."

"Princess?" Tara asked. "Why would he want to rescue me?"

"Not you," Pal said. "Some old lady. Princess Oriel."

Confounded, Tara said, "There is no princess here. Father, what is he talking about?"

Il i'Tir rose from his throne and flew over to Pal in two beats of his wings. He landed between his daughter and the rogue. "Where is he?" the dragon growled.

Pal sucked his teeth and said, "I'm afraid he's dead."

"Dead?! How?"

"I killed him," Pal said and could tell he impressed the dragon. "And boy, was it messy! You see, Cole wasn't alone. He brought some friends with him. Hikari Musha the paladin, Macario the wizard. And the captain of the elven rangers, excuse me, I mean the elven princess."

"Domina," Tara grit the name between clenched teeth.

"Yeah, I can't stand her either," Pal said. "Anyway, what's worse is it's not those heroic fools you have to deal with. As we speak, the Locksmiths Guild raids your treasury."

"How do you know all this?" Tara asked.

Pal unbuttoned his shirt and revealed his tattoo. "I'm a founding member."

Il i'Tir slithered back to his throne and ran a claw over the Eye of Nero. It filled with images of the Locksmiths plundering the treasury. "He speaks the truth!" Il i'Tir exclaimed, shocked. He was so focused on spying on his crimson nemesis, he had not prepared for an intrusion of his secret lair.

"Seize him!" Tara shouted, and in seconds, sylvan soldiers surrounded Pal, the tips of their swords at his neck.

Tara approached the throne, knelt, and said, "Let me bring you the heads of these intruders."

Il i'Tir stared into the orb at Hikari. His paw ran up his severed horn. "Bring them alive. I want to have a little fun with them."

Tara bowed and exited followed by several sylvan soldiers.

The dragon looked up from the orb and asked, "Tell me, rogue. Why do you betray your friends?"

Pal snorted and said, "I have no friends."

CHAPTER THIRTY-THREE

Third Chances

Below in the dragon's treasury, the Locksmiths filled their packs with countless sums of glittering coins. They adorned themselves with priceless gems, gold rings, sapphire necklaces, emerald bracelets, and ruby earrings. Sarik shifted the platinum crown he wore to a more comfortable position on his bald head and shouted, "Let's move!"

Fellit nodded his long ears in the direction of Hikari, Domina, Macario, and Maisie, and asked, "What about them?"

"We have no use for them anymore," Sarik said. "Kill them!"

"Okay, wizy-wiz," Maisie whispered. "How about a spell to get us out of this?"

Macario whispered back, "Aside from prestidigitation, there are few spells I have memorized verbatim. Shrinking, growth, retrieval, levitation, and transformation spells I know like the back of my hand. But if I misspeak the arcane words of a more complex spell, I might cast the wrong one, and that could have cataclysmic consequences."

"Who cares? How can things get any worse?" Maisie asked.

"Trust me. Things can always get worse."

The Locksmith's each chose a hero to kill. Rhonda chose Hikari, Fellit chose Domina, Pete-Pete chose Macario, and Rukis chose Maisie. They raised their swords, ready to deliver their death sentences.

An empty shell, Hikari always imagined he'd die with honor in battle, not in shameful captivity. He turned to Macario, Domina, and Maisie. He spoke with as much compassion as he could muster. "It was an honor knowing you." He bowed his head and prayed.

Maisie whispered, "Put in a good word for me."

Domina's violent heartbeat made her worry her heart might leap out of her chest and flee. *So this is what it's like to know you are going to die*, she thought.

An hour earlier, Markos and Falor dropped the slain sylvan door guards into the sewers. The bodies plummeted twenty feet and landed with harsh thuds and ear-splitting cracks. Stupid and evil, a wicked combination, both men winced and laughed.

"Let's grab the big lug, toss him, and head down to the treasury," Markos said.

Falor laughed and said, "I hope they left enough jewels for us. I'd like me one of those shiny king hats."

"It's called a tiara, you idiot," Markos said and smacked Falor upside the head.

"I knew that!" Falor exclaimed, rubbed his sore skull, and pouted.

"Sure," Markos said, rolling his eyes.

The two dimwits stopped when they reached the bramble tower's entrance. Falor stared at the grass confused. He asked Markos, "Where did you move the other guy?"

"What guy?"

"The big blond guy Pal killed."

"I didn't move him!"

"Well, I didn't move him."

"Neither of you moved me."

Markos and Falor turned to see Cole standing behind them, cracking his knuckles.

"But you're dead!" Markos exclaimed.

Cole raised an eyebrow and said, "Not really."

Falor gasped. A horrific thought dawned on him. "If you're dead, but not dead, that means..."

Markos was on the same wavelength as his moronic counterpart and shouted, "He's a zombie!" They wailed like sopranos and ran away crying. Cole watched them run to the open manhole he had used to go under the labyrinth. Markos fell in and Falor jumped after him, figuring it was better to die with a friend than have your brain eaten.

Cole wasn't a zombie. If anything, he was a possum. The knife Pal plunged into his chest was the enchanted twig Macario gave him in the Endless Forest. Cole touched the sore spot on his chest where the twig punctured his skin. He wondered why Pal would fake his murder? *It must be part of his plan, but what was his plan and why didn't he tell anyone about it?* All Pal said was, good luck saving the princess.

"That's it!"

Cole clapped his hand over his mouth when he realized he spoke out loud. Pal must have realized there was no way Cole could save Princess Oriel if he was captured by the Locksmiths. Cole smiled and thought, *Pal must have known the thieves followed us the whole time. That's why he voted for me to stay behind. He saved me. But why didn't he save the others?* Cole decided to get the answer to that question later. Right now, he had things to do. Heroic things!

Cole took a deep breath and climbed down the ladder into the sewers. Even holding his breath, the stench overpowered him. At the foot of the ladder, he found the bodies of Markos and Falor on top of two sylvan guards. He rolled them off the guards and tried to discern which sylvan was closest to his size. They were both short and thin, so Cole took armor from both, dressing with whatever fit best. If he hadn't starved in the elven prison, he would have been too chubby to fit in either guard's armor. *I guess there's a bright side to everything*, he thought.

Cole wished he had a mirror. For the first time in his life, he owned a suit of armor. True, it was snug, but he bet he looked pretty snazzy. Now, all he needed was a weapon.

Floating in a stream of filth, he found a sylvan longsword. He cleaned it with Falor's shirt and tucked into his belt. He named the sword Steel Reaper. Dressed in his sylvan suit of armor, he climbed out of the sewers and entered the bramble tower.

Though empty, the tower's entrance hall reeked of death. The floor was spotted with blood, the work of the Locksmiths. Cole followed the bloody trail to a closet. He opened the door and his suspicions were confirmed. The ghastly sight of three mutilated sylvan soldiers crammed inside. Cole covered his mouth and backed away.

An enormous woman, clad in black armor and a minotaur helmet, came down the wooden staircase. She led a group of sylvan soldiers and stopped in front of Cole.

"Why are you not at your post?" Tara asked.

Cole tried not to panic. Afraid he might give himself away if he spoke, he pointed to the dead sylvan soldier he found.

Tara removed her helmet and waves of jade hair splashed out of the black metal. She brushed the hair out of her eyes, behind her ears. She had fair skin, full lips, high cheekbones, and emerald eyes. She was the most enchanting sight Cole had ever seen. In an instant, he fell irrevocably in love with her.

Tara took in the situation and turned her attention to Cole. His heart skipped a beat.

"There are thieves in the treasury," she said.

"I know."

She looked at him suspicious. "How do you know?"

"Well...I, um...I figured if there were thieves here they would probably be in the treasury...stealing stuff." Cole let out a nervous laugh.

Tara looked him up and down. Cole felt exposed and vulnerable, so he tried to act casual, placing his hands on his hips and then at his side. He settled on one hand on his hip, figuring that looked best.

"You don't look like the other sylvan," Tara said.

Cole started to sweat. "That's because...I, uh...I'm only half-sylvan."

Tara noted his pale skin and blond hair. His ears were round and his frame was larger than any sylvan she'd seen before. Still, she knew what it meant to be a so-called "half-blood" and that connection led her to believe him.

"Princess Tara," one of her guards said. "Shouldn't we head to the treasury? The longer we wait, the more we increase their chance of escape."

Tara pursed her lips. "I'm sorry," she said. "Am I wasting your time?"

The sylvan, who thought he was helping, regretted speaking. "No. Of course not," he said. "I just thought..."

"Oh. You were thinking?" Tara said, grabbed him by the neck, lifted him off the ground, and crushed his windpipe.

Cole had to catch his breath. She was the most powerful being he had ever seen. Tara tossed the soldier into the closet with the rest of the dead sylvans.

"What are you staring at?" she asked Cole.

"Who? Me? Nothing. I, umm...gee...hmm...what a night, huh?" he stammered. His cheeks flushed red and his heart fluttered in his chest.

Tara shook her head in disgust. She loathed admirers. She was a warrior with no time in her schedule for love. She put her Minotaur helmet back on. "Anyone else have any thoughts?" No one said a word. "Good. Follow me."

CHAPTER THIRTY-FOUR

The Final Betrayal

Cole and the sylvan soldiers followed Tara into the treasury. They found Hikari, Macario, Maisie, and Domina, a sword's stroke away from death. Tara held up a clenched fist outside the open doorway and the soldiers came to a halt. Cole looked at the frightening barbed walls and ceiling and missed the signal. He bumped into the sylvan in front of him, who in turn shot him a nasty glare.

He heard Rhonda ask, "Any last words?"
Hikari replied in a singsong rhythm,
"Since days of eld, till nights unmet,
We the chosen will never set.
We worship your light, heat, and power,
And call upon you in our darkest hour.

"Rey, shine down on me and my companions for we have come to our journey's conclusion and the end of our days. May we enjoy an eternity within your light and join our fallen friends."

Solemn, Domina thought of her mother. Macario and Maisie shared a bleak smiled. Their friendship was brief but exciting.

Tara drew her boomerang blade, calculated the trajectory, and threw it. The blade hummed in the air. Four pauses in its deadly song cut off the raised hands of Rhonda, Fellit, Pete-

Pete, and Rukis. A second later, the boomerang blade was back in Tara's hand and the sylvan soldiers stormed in.

Cole let the others do the killing. Still undercover, he held back and kept out of sight from his friends. The sylvans slayed the human Locksmiths. They refused to attack Fellit and Rukis (the elf and gnome) because they were Fair Folk. So Tara executed them. Sarik was spared as he raised his hands in surrender. Tara shoved him toward Cole, who shackled him with much satisfaction.

Tara triumphantly surveyed each member of the captured party. She came to Domina, removed her helmet and said, "Why is it every time we meet, elf, you always end up beneath my blade? This time, daddy isn't here to safe you."

Domina spat at her. Tara wiped the white foam from her breastplate. She looked at the spit hanging from her gloved fingers with disdain, said, "How unbecoming of an elf."

"Mud'hir Erta will spit you out after your traitorous sylvan servants dig your grave."

Tara replied with a vicious right hook, landing square across Domina's face. A welt darkened around Domina's eye. Uncontrollable tears ran down her cheeks, leaving clean trails through the dirt.

"Princess Tara," one of the soldiers said, and presented her with the unicorn's horn she found in Domina's backpack.

Tara's eyes shone with emerald fire. "The horn!" she exclaimed. "Finally, it's mine. With this, Hexor's defeat is all but certain."

Out of the corner of her eye, Tara saw Macario blinking and nodding his head around the room. She glared at the wizard, he smiled back innocently. *Wizards! You never know what they're up to,* she thought, but said, "Take the prisoners to my father!"

A guard shackled Maisie's torso in one cuff and attached the other to Macario's ankle.

"Is it me or do you guys get caught a lot?" she asked.

Cole decided he would wait for the appropriate time to reveal himself and his gut told him now was not that time.

One by one, Tara presented the shackled heroes and Sarik to the dragon. Il i'Tir sat on his throne, his legs curled beneath him like a cat and his chest puffed out with pride. His claws tapped the arm of his throne with a cruel beat.

"What an unexpected surprise to see you again, paladin," the dragon said. "Don't get too comfortable. I'm afraid your stay won't be long."

Tara stepped forward, knelt, and bowed her head. "Father," she said. "I have disarmed the intruders and bring you these gifts."

A procession of sylvan soldiers offered what they had confiscated. Il i'Tir announced each with increasing delight.

"A sylvan-made staff. A ranger's swords and bow. And," he said and raised the Sun Sword in his claw, a dagger to a dragon, "a paladin's sword! These will be fine additions to my collection." Hikari chuckled. "What are you laughing at, paladin?"

"Only the pure of heart may wield the Sun Sword, dragon. You have sealed your own doom."

"A strong boast from one who stands powerless before me."

Tara knelt at her father's feet and offered her final gift.

"A unicorn horn," Il i'Tir gasped. He delicately took the horn in his clutch and closed his eyes, basking in its power. "Tara, no words could describe how proud I am of you. You have not only proved yourself worthy of your bloodline, you have carved out your own place in history. Well done daughter."

Tara nodded, but inside she beamed with pride.

"Unwittingly, my guests brought me the one weapon that will defeat my crimson nemesis and usher in the reign of Il i'Tir."

"Not if we have anything to say about it," Hikari barked.

Even in the face of certain death, Hikari's bravery was unmatched. The dragon rolled his yellow eyes and brought his snout and inch from Hikari's nose. "You are shackled, weaponless, and, by the smell of it," he sniffed Hikari, "wounded. Your threats are a joke. How could you ever defeat me?"

"The power of Rey, god of light, truth, and justice never strays from my side."

"Yes, yes," the dragon mocked. "But where is your god now? Why does he not save you?"

"You'll be called to answer him soon enough," Hikari said, his eyes stabbing the beast through the soul.

"I tire of these petty threats. Rogue!" Pal stepped from behind a pillar. "As per our agreement, I will let you live if you pledge your allegiance to me."

"Just when I thought you couldn't stoop any lower!" Domina shouted.

Tara shoved Domina to the hard grassy floor. She pressed her foot down on her spine. "Quiet, elf."

The dragon held the Sun Sword out to Pal. "Strike down the paladin and solidify our pact."

Pal nodded, took the sword, and walked toward Hikari. Slow. Methodical. A hangman approaching the gallows.

Cole was shocked to see Pal playing the executioner. During the time Cole was presumed dead, a lot had transpired and little of it made sense to him. It took an immense amount of self-control to not leap into action. It looked bad, but Cole trusted Pal completely. He was his best friend after all. Sure, Pal was a thief, but he wasn't a killer. If he was, he would have let Sarik and his cronies kill him at the Drunken Skeleton. There was more to Pal than what was seen on the surface, same as it was with Cole. This had to be a part of Pal's master plan.

Pal lowered the katana to Hikari's neck. He gazed into his eyes and saw the contempt and distrust he held for him since day one.

"Please. Don't do it," Domina pleaded. "There must be some good in you."

Pal raised the Sun Sword. Cole held his breath. Hikari bowed his head, ready to die.

"I'm sorry, Domina. I'm no good. I am, and have always been, a traitor," Pal said and brought down the divine katana.

Broken chain links dangled from Hikari's shackles. He looked up into Pal's eyes with crow's feet at their corners. The arrogant eyes grinned, and for the first time, Hikari saw the good buried deep within the rogue. Pal offered him the Sun Sword. Hikari smiled and took his sword. The blade radiated in the hands of its master.

Pal turned to Il i'Tir and said, "Never trust a thief."

The dragon roared, rallying his army. Throughout the tower, goblins cringed. Worried their master may punish them, they left their stations and ran to his aid.

"Now, dragon," Hikari said twirling his sword. "You will answer to me."

Tara screamed at the sylvan soldiers, "Kill them!" The sylvans held their ground. "I ordered you to kill them."

Adrias, the sylvan lieutenant, stepped forward. "This has gone far enough. The cost of allying with one dragon to defeat another is too high. We will not bare arms against an elf, especially their princess."

Domina smiled with her eyes. Enraged, Tara trembled. "Oath breakers."

The soldiers formed a wall, protecting the prisoners. Hikari slashed the air and sent a solar flare that melted his friends' shackles.

"What about me?" Sarik asked, still bound in iron.

"I didn't forget about you," Pal said and socked Sarik in the face.

The goblin reinforcements arrived. Hundreds ran into the throne room and flanked the party. Tara rushed at Adrias and the sylvan traitors. She struck with her boomerang blade in one hand, and blocked their swords with her helmet.

Macario cast a succession of retrieval spells,

"Soar in the air to my friends,
Arm them now, Retrieve their weapons."

The Sun Sword, ironwood bow and arrows flew into Hikari's and Domina's hands. Macario caught his Sylvanus Staff in one hand and the strap of his backpack library in the other.

"Wowee!" Maisie cried. "I'm sticking with you, wizy-wiz!"

"I hoped you would say that. By any chance, would you mind if I cast a growth spell on you?"

"You mean to turn me into a giant rat so you can ride on my back like a horse?"

"I imagined something more like an elephant."

Maisie smiled. "Let's do it."

Macario spoke the arcane rhyme,

"Little friend, it's time to grow,
Ten times your size, come now show."

Maisie grew, much to the horror of the onlooking goblins. She wrapped her tail around Macario's waist and lifted him onto her back.

"Hold on tight," she said.

He complied. Maisie stood on her hind legs and roared. She plowed through a dozen goblins, crushing them under her weight. Macario hooted with joy. He knew he had found his familiar.

Hikari approached the dragon, cutting down goblins in his path. "Your reign of terror ends tonight, Il i'Tir."

The dragon growled and whipped his tail at Hikari. The paladin hurtled over it and stabbed the dragon in the flank. Il i'Tir writhed under the power of the holy sword.

Pal and Sarik grappled on the floor. For a man in shackles, Sarik put up a good fight. He had plenty of experience sparring with his wrists bound. He managed to catch Pal in a headlock and strangle him.

"Why are you fighting me?" Sarik asked. "While everyone is distracted, we can escape."

"No, thanks," Pal said, throwing an elbow into Sarik's ribs, which gave him a chance to slip out of the headlock.

"You're still a member of the Locksmiths," Sarik said.

"Consider this my resignation." Pal slammed his foot against the side of Sarik's head, knocking him unconscious. The rogue stood, dusted himself off, and looked for Domina.

Domina retrieved her ironwood swords, bow, and quiver of arrows. She began picking off the advancing goblins. Hearing heavy footsteps behind her, she turned and nocked another arrow.

The sylvan soldier stopped dead in his tracks. "Don't shoot!"

Domina lowered her bow. She couldn't believe her eyes. "Cole?!"

His name resounded above the fighting. Macario and Maisie cheered and waved. Pal smirked. He knew he could count on Cole. Hikari was in total shock. For a second, he forgot he was engaged in battle and let his guard down, allowing Il i'Tir to rake his claws across his chest. Hikari growled in agony. There would be time for celebrating later. Right now, there was a dragon to slay.

Domina hugged Cole and exclaimed, "I can't believe it! You're alive!"

"Of course I am. Pal would never hurt me. I'm his best friend. It was a fake out. All part of his master plan."

Domina looked over at Pal battling a pack of goblins. All she presumed about him the past hour was wrong. Her heart skipped a beat.

Cole said, "He's a pretty great guy, isn't he?"

"He sure is something." Domina fired six successive shots and killed the goblins surrounding Pal.

Daggers in each hand, he dashed over to them and said, "I knew you wouldn't let me down, Cole."

"I knew you would never betray me."

Domina fired an arrow between them, killing a stray goblin. "When you two boys are done with your romance, I could use a little help."

"Go save the princess," Pal told Cole. "She's at the top of the tower."

"How do you know?"

"They're always at the top of the tower. You're not the only one who likes stories," Pal said with a wink.

"Can you handle this?" Cole asked, gazing across the room at Tara battling sylvans.

"This is your best shot to save her," Pal said. "Everyone will be focused on the fight in here, so you shouldn't have any trouble. Domina and I will block the staircase so you'll be safe as you head to the top. Got it, Cole? Cole?"

Domina snapped her fingers in front of his face and said, "Focus on the mission, Cole."

"Right. Get the princess. Get out of here. Get fortune and glory." Cole said, regaining his concentration. Still, his eyes drifted toward the half-dragon princess.

Pal sighed, and said, "Go, lover boy."

Cole inhaled a deep breath and unleashed a psychotic battle cry. He ran out of the room swinging the Steel Reaper at the goblins pouring into the throne room. Domina and Pal looked at each other. Taking a page out of Cole's book, they unleashed their own battle cry and ran headfirst into the onslaught of goblins.

CHAPTER THIRTY-FIVE

Rescuing the Princess

Eighty flights of stairs later, Cole's thighs and glutes on fire, he made it to the top landing. He leaned on Princess Oriel's door, trying to catch his breath. He knocked and a moment later, heard movement within, but no reply. He knocked again. Louder.

"It's too soon. I haven't recovered from the last feeding," a timid voice came from behind the door.

"Princess Oriel?" Cole asked between breaths.

"Yes?"

"My name...is Cole. Your father...King Langsley...sent me...to rescue you. Can I please...come in? I'm exhausted."

After a brief pause he heard a chair moved from under the doorknob on the other side. The door creaked open and Cole looked down at the wrinkled woman who used to be Princess Oriel. All her beauty and grace had been lost to decades of solitude. Her ginger hair was graying and her eyes were a cloudy blue. The crown atop her head was dull and unpolished. Wire-rimmed spectacles rested on her plump nose. Her drooping jowls make her look like a frog. She did not look anything like the beautiful young girl in her portrait.

Princess Oriel's eyes darted up and down Cole. "There has not been a hero to rescue me in some forty years," she said.

"Sorry for the delay," Cole said, looking past her into the room. "Is that a chair? I could use a good sit down."

"No one ever comes into the room, except for the goblins who feed me and... him."

"Right. As soon as I get a few minutes to rest, I'll be ready to escort you out of the tower and take you home."

"Home." Princess Oriel said in a distant voice, took a few steps back, and allowed Cole to enter her bedchamber. "Home," she repeated and guffawed, shaking her head.

Princess Oriel had hoarded forty years worth of garbage in the dark bedroom. Stacks upon stacks of books and drawings and poems and paintings. Used kerchiefs, pillow feathers, and dinner scraps piled around her bed. Marbles were strewn across the floor, caltrops.

Cole waded through the aisles of trash to the chair near her standing mirror. He stabbed the Steel Reaper into the floor and used it as a crutch to lower himself into the chair. With an exaggerated sigh, Cole exhaled all the day's exhaustion and enjoyed the reprieve.

Princess Oriel paced back and forth. The truth was she had not had a visitor in her bedchamber for over forty years. All her most private and personal possessions were out in the open for him to judge.

"The truth is, for the past forty years, I haven't left this room. I can't leave this room. This is my home now. I like it here."

Cole looked around the dim messy room and said, "Are you sure you're not a little nervous? I know you've been cooped up here for a long time, but it's time to go home."

Princess Oriel blurted an unsettling laugh and waved Cole's suggestion away. "My father is but a distant memory." She gathered her most important, soiled kerchiefs, afraid he might try to steal them.

"Trust me. He cares about you. I care."

"Ha. No one cares about me. No one but Il. He brings me gifts. He visits me when I'm lonely. He loves me and he never wants to hurt me but sometimes I act out. All he asks is for a little blood and I've got more than enough to share. No. I'm not leaving. I won't go."

"Listen, you're the first princess I've rescued. It would be a little embarrassing for me to make it all the way to the end of the journey and not bring you home. I swear no harm will come to you. You've got to come with me."

"I appreciate the kind words, but I am too old to up and leave. I have made a life here. My adulthood was not what I imagined it would be when I was but a girl, but life is like a marble."

"Round?"

"Hard. Sometimes fun, but most of the time it feels like it is getting away from you."

"Okay, Princess Oriel. You've definitely been a prisoner in this tower way too long."

The Princess crouched behind an easel. The painting displayed a still life of an apple and bottle of nectar. On the writing desk beside the painting were the same apple, now a rotted core, and the empty bottle of nectar.

"I'm not leaving and you can't make me!"

Cole looked at Princess Oriel with disdain and thought, *are you kidding me? I climbed up a mile of stairs, and now you don't want to even be rescued?! What is wrong with these royals?!* In a calculated delivery, he said, "I promised your father I would bring you home and a hero always keeps his promise. So stop horsing around and let's go!"

Princess Oriel folded her arms, scrunched her nose like a defiant teenage girl, and shouted, "No!"

"I'm too tired to argue with you," Cole said. "So, here's the deal. I'm going to count to three, and if you don't come with me on your own, I'm going to carry you. Okay?"

"Why don't we stay here and have a pot of tea?"

"One..."

"I can read you some poetry."

"Two..."

Princess Oriel stepped behind a tower of romance novels. She picked up a hardcover book and held it up, ready to throw it at Cole. "You keep your hands off me."

"Three!"

She threw the hardcover book at him and hit him square on the nose. Cole cursed and chased Princess Oriel around the room like a loose hen. Cole slipped on a marble, his feet flew up in the air, and he landed flat on his back. Princess Oriel laughed at him.

Cole closed his eyes and let the mocking laughter rain over him. He began this journey unqualified, inexperienced, and unappreciated. But his whole life he'd been desperate to jump at the call to adventure. His impetuous, overeager attitude and stubbornness got him into trouble far too often. If he continued in this manner, he knew he would never achieve the success he always dreamed of. It was time to think outside the box. Time to use the rules as guidelines. Time to make a plan. Time to trust his instincts.

"Fine," Cole said. "You don't want to leave. You can stay here. Stay here the rest of your life. I'll bring your daughter back instead. I'm sure King Langsley will pay me the reward for his granddaughter."

"My daughter?" Princess Oriel asked, peeking from behind her bed.

Cole stood, brushed indented marbles off his back, and said, "You know, Princess Tara. The half-dragon. I don't know why you ever agreed to marry a dragon in the first place. Although Il i'Tir is charming in a horrible sort of way."

Princess Oriel crawled over the bed to Cole. "My daughter is alive?"

"Yeah, and you're identical. Except she's young. And pretty."

Princess Oriel unleashed a primal scream. She kicked over the easel, and stomped on a still life painting, pushing her foot through an acrylic pear. "That bloody dragon lied to me. All those years ago, he told she was stillborn."

"One thing I've learned about dragons is they lie a lot," Cole said.

"Take me to my daughter."

"Okay, but you have to promise to go back to Castle Langsley with me so I can get my reward."

"Yes, yes," Princess Oriel said throwing a stained shawl over her shoulders. "It's about time I give that dragon a piece of my mind."

The old woman hurried out of the room and down the stairs, invigorated by her mission.

Cole chased after her and called, "Wait for me!"

CHAPTER THIRTY-SIX

Family Reunion

Cole and Princess Oriel navigated the long, steep, winding staircase. As they descended, the sounds of battle grew louder and Cole got excited. He may not miss all the action, after all.

He was a flight ahead of Princess Oriel, who lagged behind wheezing. Hearing the roar of battle echo from below, he couldn't wait any longer and shouted, "Come on, Princess!" He ran back up the stairs, lifted her in his arms, and carried her down the rest of the way.

"My word!" Princess Oriel exclaimed. "I have not had such excitement in a witch's age!"

Cole raced down the stairs, the middle-aged princess in his arms.

The tower was a congested battlefield. Tara fought the sylvans, their numbers dwindling under her boomerang blade. Macario and Maisie circled the perimeter of the throne room, gleefully bulldozing goblins. Hikari dueled with Il i'Tir, parrying his claws and tail as only a master swordsman could.

Pal and Domina fended off the goblins on the stairs. They fought as a unit. Domina ran out of arrows and swatted a charging goblin with her bow. Pal lifted a sword from the ground with his foot, whistled, and kicked it to Domina. She caught the sword in her free hand and plunged it into a goblin's chest.

"Thank you," she said and unsheathed her ironwood swords. Pal flashed her a disarming smile. She pushed the button on the hilt of her sword and its twin fell into her open hand. She pointed it at him. "That doesn't mean I forgive you."

A hobgoblin shoveled dead goblins aside and came at Domina. It snapped its jaws at her neck. Pal hurled a dagger into its open mouth and the huge beast toppled over. Another wave of goblins came. Pal and Domina parried each attack and conversed as if they were alone.

"I'm sorry," Pal shouted over the clatter of battle. "I should have told you my plan sooner."

"In a life and death situation, all you can think about is the apologizing?" Domina asked and impaled a goblin through the belly, " I think you have a crush on me."

Pal grabbed a leaping goblin, plunged his dagger into its chest, and said, "I wanted you to know, in case we die."

"No one dies today," Domina said.

Together, they fought until the goblins were no more.

Tara whittled away until the only sylvan left was Adrias. He advanced with his longsword, piercing it through her helmet's visor. Having trapped his sword, she threw her boomerang blade. It flew past him and then arced around and plunged into his back. His expression froze and he fell at her feet. Tara retrieved the blade and wiped it clean with his cape.

Hikari backed Il i'Tir up against his throne and stabbed the dragon's wing, rendering it useless. Relentlessly, Hikari thrashed the dragon and drew blood. Il i'Tir lost his balance and fell backward and destroying his throne. The Eye of Nero hit the floor, shattered, and scrying magic hissed out of the glass shards. The unicorn's horn rolled under the rubble. Still, Hikari came for him.

Il i'Tir was on the brink of death and cowered before the paladin. One clean strike would be enough to decapitate the foul creature.

Hikari channeled his remaining pool of divine energy into the Sun Sword. The blade burned blinding white and was hot enough to liquefy anything it touched. Gripping the hilt with both hands, Hikari rushed at the dragon, and shouted, "For Rey!" The Sun Sword swept through the air, leaving sparks in its trail.

Tara smashed into Hikari's side. She knocked the wind out of him and cracked a rib. Wincing, Hikari grabbed his side. His divine power drained, he could not heal himself.

Standing between the paladin and her wounded father, Tara raised the boomerang blade. But before she could throw it, Cole entered with Princess Oriel in his arms.

"Il!" she shouted at the top of her lungs.

The chaos in the room came to a halt. As soon as she saw Princess Oriel's face, Tara went numb. She turned her father, suspicious a terrible secret was about to be revealed. "Who is that?" she whispered.

Princess Oriel made her way to the dragon, "You lied to me. All these years you lied to me. You called me your love. You told me you needed to keep me safe, safe from the world. But that wasn't true, was it?

"All you ever wanted from me was my blood, to infuse you with its royal power. And like a fool I believed you. When you asked me to, I paid that grim price for my safety because I trusted you. I trusted you! And now, after all I've given, I come to find you have kept my daughter a secret?"

"Mother?!" Tara gasped.

Princess Oriel wept tears of both joy and agony. "Yes, my daughter. Your mother lives."

"But my mother died giving birth to me."

"Another lie." Princess Oriel took her daughter's hand in hers.

Tara's knees buckled. Overcome by a new and vulnerable sensation—doubt. She released the old woman's hands and stepped behind her father.

"No. It can't be true. Father said it was a witch he held prisoner at the top of the tower."

"A witch was I?"

The dragon shrugged. "Semantics."

Macario steered Maisie over to Hikari and helped him onto her back.

"Are you okay?" Macario asked.

"I have suffered great pains, but the day is not done. We must regroup and form a plan," the paladin said.

"Right. Maisie, take us to the others."

"Yep, yep!" she exclaimed and galloped over to Cole, Pal, and Domina. Macario and Hikari dismounted. Macario changed Maisie back to her normal size.

"Who's in favor of getting out of here while the getting is good?" Pal asked.

Maisie raised her pink hand.

"What about her?" Cole asked and nodded at Tara.

"I say we leave them while they're still bickering," Pal said.

"We can't leave her," Cole said.

"You're right. She must stand trial for her crimes against my people," Domina said.

"I doubt she'll come as willingly as Princess Oriel," Macario said.

Domina agreed. "Give me one of those mushrooms from the garden, Cole."

"How can you think of food at a time like this?"

"Just do it."

"Okay," Cole said and handed her a mushroom from his backpack and thought, *I'll never understand elves.*

Domina took the mushroom. She retrieved an arrow from a goblin corpse. The party watched the horrific family reunion unfold.

Princess Oriel held out her hand. "Come with me Tara. Come home to Redlund."

Tara froze. How could she leave her father, who raised her to be a warrior and gave her an army, to live with a woman, no, a stranger? For the first time in her life she was indecisive.

Il i'Tir's yellow eyes widened. "Insolent witch! The girl is mine."

"So it is true?" Tara asked.

"I had to keep you from her. A mother would have taught you kindness and love, and that would have made you weak."

"Those are the qualities that make you strong," Hikari said.

"Don't listen to them Tara. They are trying to corrupt you. Remember who loves you. Your place is at my side. Your destiny is to help me defeat Hexor so I can save the world."

Cole laughed. "I don't think so. I'm destined to fall in love with the one who will save the world. And frankly, you're not my type."

"I don't know what to believe anymore," Tara said.

"Listen to your mother," Princess Oriel said. "It's time to go home."

Tara made her decision. "I'm sorry. I am home."

Il i'Tir smiled, triumphant.

"The decision isn't yours." Domina speared the mushroom, nocked the arrow, aimed, and fired at Tara. The mushroom exploded on Tara's black breastplate emitting poisonous spores. Tara inhaled them and lost control of reality. She fell and Cole caught her. He smiled and wrapped his arms around her.

"We have her. Now, make haste!" Princess Oriel commanded. They turned and ran for the exit.

Il i'Tir's rage gave him the strength to propel himself one last time. He snatched Princess Oriel and gobbled her up. Cole was aghast. One second he tasted victory, having rescued the princess, the next, she was an hors d'oeuvre. Il i'Tir regurgitated Princess Oriel. She was nothing more than a steaming skeleton. Pal picked up her crown and stored it in his pack.

Princess Oriel's royal blood empowered the dragon and renewed his strength. He mended his wing with dark magic and sealed his wounds.

"Come, dragon," Hikari said brandishing the glowing Sun Sword, "Atone for your crimes at the edge of my blade."

Il i'Tir dug up the unicorn horn from under the rubble of his throne. "I've come too far to let you stop me now. Behold, the true power of the unicorn." He raised the horn above his head, and plunged it into his heart.

A shockwave sent the group flying to the other side of the room against a wall hidden in black smoke. *Thump. Thump. Thump.* The dragon stomped through the smoke engulfed in crackling purple energy.

The color drained from Macario's face. "Oh, no," he said. "He's using the horn as an equus shield."

"What's that?" Cole asked.

"An ancient spell originally cast by the legendary..."

Pal interrupted Macario. "The short version, please!"

Macario was pale. He looked at his comrades.

"Any blow we land will heal him. He's... invincible."

CHAPTER THIRTY-SEVEN

Mad Dash

The dragon flapped his wings and soared above the throne room. He struck the ceiling with his tail, sending down a storm of deadly thorns. An enormous wooden spike separated Cole and Hikari from the others. Tara lay incapacitated near them, mumbling about her mother.

Hikari grabbed Cole and said, "Take the others and get out of here."

"Heroes never run from a battle," Cole said.

"Yes they do, and the time for you to run is now. You must save the princess, Cole. Bring her home safe before her father can corrupt her anymore. Her redemption is paramount. If you don't save her from herself, our quest has been for naught."

Pal shouted from the doorway, "Cole! Let's go!"

Cole looked into the hazel eyes of his friend and said, "I don't want to leave you. I want to stay and fight with you. I want to be brave."

Hikari smiled. "You are brave. That was never a question." Cole's heart swelled. "You need to lead the party to safety. I can give you more time."

Cole's eyes widened. "Lead?"

Hikari nodded. "You are ready."

Cole melted under the heat of the compliment. Earning Hikari's trust was his life's greatest accomplishment.

"Fine, but I better see you again."

"You will."

"Cole!" Pal shouted, waving from the doorway.

"Go!" Hikari exclaimed.

Cole lifted Tara over his shoulder and met Pal at the door. Hikari turned to the dragon, brandishing the glowing Sun Sword. The dragon roared and equus sparks burst from his jaws. Both charged one another; the forces of good and evil collided.

Cole led the party out of the bramble tower, carrying Tara. They crossed the goblin breeding grounds safely. At the labyrinth's entrance, Pal got shot in the calf by an arrow. Domina dashed to his side and helped him to his feet. In the distance, Sarik, free of his shackles, reloaded a crossbow and fired another arrow at Pal. Domina caught the arrow on the belly of her bow.

Sarik reloaded the crossbow again. "There is no where you can run or hide from me Pal. I will never give up until you're dead."

"Well, you have to admit, he's determined," Pal said to Domina.

"We have to keep moving," Cole said.

"Pal's injured," Domina said.

"I'm fine," Pal lied. "But we should keep moving. I don't think Sarik is as forgiving as you."

"You're still on my short list," Domina said.

"Follow me," Maisie said. "There's an entrance to the sewers nearby. We can hide there."

"No. We go back the way we came," Cole said.

Maisie protested, "But I told you…"

"I know what you told me!" Cole shouted. "You all have to trust me."

The party ran through the labyrinth. Cole carried Tara. Domina carried Pal. Macario carried Maisie. And Sarik pursed, carrying his crossbow.

Running at full speed, Cole led them forward.

"He's going to get us lost!" Domina shouted. "This is suicide!"

"The paths keep changing!" Macario cried.

"Exactly," Cole said. "This labyrinth doesn't play fair, does it, Maisie?"

The rat's whiskers bristled and Macario was sure Maisie smiled at him. "It sure doesn't. Nope, nope."

"If you turn around, it leads you right back to the beginning," Cole said, quoting the rodent.

It worked. The walls shifted and the paths directed them back to the courtyard outside of the labyrinth; the gate to Elfwood before them.

"Great," Pal said. "Here we are at the beginning. But there is a cave full of angry pixies on the other side of the gate. Remember?"

"I do," Cole said.

"So how are we going to get out?" Domina asked.

"Let me think," Cole said.

Another arrow sailed past Pal's head and he glanced over his shoulder. Sarik gained on them. "Think faster," Pal said.

"Think outside the box," Cole said to himself. He snapped, "Macario!"

"Yes?"

"You're going to fly us out," Cole said.

"We went over this already. I can't fly."

"I know. I know. But you can levitate. Everyone, grab onto Macario. And when I tell you to, Macario, cast your levitation spell."

Sarik breached the courtyard. Revenge in his eyes, he loaded the crossbow once more and took aim.

The party grabbed hold of Macario. "Not so tight," the wizard complained. "I can barely breathe."

Sarik fired another arrow and it sunk into Pal's back. He howled in pain. A little to the left and it would have struck his spine. Sarik cursed, dropped the crossbow, and drew a short sword. Growling, he charged the party.

"Now, Macario! Cast the levitation spell! Everyone else, lean him forward."

The party held Macario at a ninety degree angle. They aimed him at the gate. He recited the arcane rhyme to the levitation spell,

"Sylvanus Staff, raise me now,
High as a raven in the clouds."

They shot through the air like an arrow. Sarik swung his sword and nipped Pal's back.

Pal looked back and saw Sarik curse and take his anger out on the walls of the labyrinth. A bad idea. The labyrinth's dryad returned, fury in her acorn eyes.

"Those who harm my garden face my wrath," she thundered.

The last Pal saw of Sarik was him disappearing into her thorned grasp.

They clung to Macario for dear life. They flew past The Void's gate, through the pixie cave, and out of the Rainbow Falls. They make a less than graceful landing on the other side of the riverbank.

"It worked!" Cole exclaimed, laughing. "I can't believe that worked!"

They rejoiced in a mosh pit of enthusiasm and surprise.

For the first time, Pal saw Domina's dazzling smile. He forgot about the arrow sticking out of his back, all there was in the world was her smile. In a moment of passion, Domina grabbed Pal by his black collar and pressed her lips against his. The world spun around them. When equilibrium settled, she regained her senses. They stared at each other speechless. Then she slapped him and he fell.

"Oh, come on," she said. "I didn't slap you that hard."

Pal pulled the broken arrow from his back. "Cupid got me," he said and dropped the bloody arrow and the world went black.

Domina dropped to her knees. Cursing her pride, she prayed to Mud'hir Erta he was not dead and pressed her long pointed ear to his chest. His heartbeat calmed hers. He fainted from shock. His eyes fluttered open. Pal stared up into Domina's warm azure eyes. She whispered comforting elven words to him and hoisted him up to his feet.

"Don't worry," she whispered to him. "I've got you."

Domina helped Pal to his feet, turned to the others, and said, "Pal is dying. We have to get him back to Elfwick."

Cole noticed she addressed him. In fact, they all looked to Cole for what to do next. He cleared his throat and in his best impression of Hikari said, "Alright. First to Elfwick to get Pal patched up and then back to Castle Langsley."

Still incapacitated from the mushrooms, Tara moaned. Macario read aloud from a scroll and thrust his staff in Tara's direction.

"Hear my rhyme, I'll make it clear
Entrap this villain in a sphere"

He conjured a large sphere of arcane energy and trapped her.

"Nice bubble-wubble, wizy-wiz," Maisie said.

Macario thanked the rat with a wink.

The party set off on their journey back to Langsley. Cole lagged behind, gazing at the Rainbow Falls. Macario laid a reassuring hand on his shoulder and said, "Don't worry, Cole. Hikari will be fine."

The entire waterfall exploded, and the green dragon rocketed out of it with Hikari in his arms. Allowing gravity to do the dirty work, Il i'Tir dropped Hikari a hundred feet and *splat*! Hikari, landed in front of Cole, broken and half-dead.

CHAPTER THIRTY-EIGHT

The Dragon of Elfwood

The green dragon circled above Cole and his companions and cast a shadow over them. Cole wracked his brain. A million thoughts blurred into none. He promised Hikari he would return Tara to King Langsley but he couldn't leave him alone to die. He needed to make a decision and fast.

Cole turned to the party and blurted, "Take the princess and get out of here!"

"You'll die!" Macario exclaimed.

Cole picked up the Sun Sword and said, "Not without a fight." No one moved. "Go. I'll give you whatever time I can."

"Are you sure?" Domina asked.

Cole gulped and said, "Go! Before I change my mind."

Macario nodded. He and Maisie pushed the bubble, rolling Tara into the woods. Domina and Pal limped behind.

Cole stood in front of Hikari to protect him. His body was on fire. Not nervous, but hyper aware. He burned with berserker frenzy, the war drums beating in his ears. He didn't bother to wipe away the sweat rolling down his brow into his eyes. His focus was dead set on the descending dragon.

Il i'Tir landed in front of Cole. His claws raked through the grass, leaving gruesome tracks.

"Fool," the green dragon snarled as it stomped up to Cole. "You think you can defeat me when a paladin can't?"

"I'm not afraid of you," Cole said through gritted teeth. He took the low stance Hikari taught him and raised the Sun Sword.

"You should be!" the dragon cried, thrashed its tail, and whipped the Sun Sword out of Cole's hands.

The dragon slammed a claw against Cole's chest and pinned him to the ground. All the air in his body was forced from his lungs. Stars danced in front of him, and for a second, the pain shooting up his spine disappeared. But when Cole sucked in oxygen, the pain returned. His entire body throbbed. He choked on his own breath and whimpered. He had never felt so much sheer strength before. It sobered him in an awful way.

In a final act of desperation, Cole grasped for the Sun Sword, but it was out of reach. He knew he would die. What good is a hero without a weapon? Cole had nothing.

Il i'Tir brought his snout close to Cole. Acidic mucus dripped from his nostrils and sizzled on his armor.

"Why didn't you run with the others?" the dragon asked, his murderous eyes sparkled. "You still have so much to prove don't you, Cole? And to think this all could have been avoided if you joined me. Without the power I gave you, you are worthless. A stupid weakling."

Hikari used the last of his strength to push himself up. "You're wrong. He's the bravest and most creative person I've ever met."

Cole started to cry. If he were to die, at least it would be beside the person he respected the most.

The Amulet of Mud'hir Erta given to Hikari by the elves dangled from his neck. Blood dripped from it like a full sponge.

Inspiration took hold of Cole. He reached into his coin purse and took out the Seed of Hope.

The elven queen's words came back to him. "Plant the seed, nurture it, give it time, and one day, it will blossom."

The Seed of Hope was not symbolic, it *was* Cole. The dream to become a hero was planted when he was a child. Hikari nurtured his dream by training him. Cole blossomed into the master of his destiny. Whatever he believed could be possible, would be possible. Since he didn't believe he could slay the invincible dragon, he would change him instead. The time had come to prove himself worthy of his mentor's respect.

"Now, you die," Il i'Tir said.

The dragon opened its mouth. His breath smelled like death, and Cole saw the poisonous gas swirling in the monster's throat. Globs of acidic drool fell from his bottom lip and melted the grass.

"I hope this does something," he said and threw the tiny seed into the dragon's open mouth.

Il i'Tir swallowed the seed. "Trying to ruin my appetite?" the dragon asked.

"At this point, I'm trying anything."

"Foolish boy. You should have joined me. You have sealed..." the dragon gagged, "Your doom!"

Il i'Tir choked and stumbled backward. Cole scrambled away. He watched in awe as roots and branches slithered out of the dragon's mouth and nostrils. The dragon tore at them, but on and on they grew.

"What have you done to me?" the dragon gurgled.

"You always wanted to be worshiped. Well, now I've turned you into a shrine," Cole said.

The green dragon made a final attempt to take Cole's life. He reached his massive claws toward the hero and froze. In a matter of seconds, the dragon was rooted to the ground. Cole took a few cautious steps back. He watched in awe as the Emerald Enormity transformed into a topiary statue. The dragon-plant-thing solidified with a hiss.

"Cole," Hikari called for his pupil.

"Hikari," Cole said, rushed over to his friend, and held him in his arms.

The paladin's eyes were full of tears. "Cole, my hero."

"Come on. You have to pray. Recharge your powers and heal yourself."

"No. I'm too weak."

"The equus horn!"

Cole ran over to the topiary. He plunged his hand into its chest and grasped for the horn. Thorns nipped at his fingers and drew blood but he endured the pain until he had it. The familiar grooved horn was clenched in Cole's grip. He pulled but it would not budge.

"Please," he cried.

The horn retracted and Cole fell. Within the topiary, he heard a faint rumble and whinny. The overgrowth shook violently and from its chest, burst a glorious black baby unicorn.

His mane and horn were purple, like the warlock's magic. His eyes emerald like the dragon's scales. His coat, dark as the night sky. The foal stood on his hind legs and kicked the air triumphantly.

"Thank the god," Cole exclaimed.

He stood and reached for the unicorn, but the foal was frightened by his voice and galloped away.

"No! Wait. You have to heal my friend."

But it was too late. The unicorn hid in the trees.

"Come back," Cole said.

Hikari called for his friend. Cole ran to his side and took his hand.

"Don't worry Hikari. I'll take you to the elves. They can heal you."

"Cole... I'm dying."

"Don't talk like that."

"Cole. You must do something for me. My brother, Kage, you must find him and give him the Sun Sword."

Cole cried. "You can give it to him yourself."

Hikari said with great difficulty, "He is in great danger. I have foreseen it. Somewhere in the mountains of Heaven's Peak, you will find him. Promise me. Promise me you will give him the Sun Sword."

Cole wiped a tear clinging to his nose onto his sleeve. "I promise."

"And tell him... I'm sorry."

Hikari's eyes lost focus. He exhaled a final breath and his spirit left his body. Cole held his friend. The black unicorn cautiously revealed himself. He watched the humans with curiosity. Above, the clouds parted and a ray of sunlight shone down on them.

CHAPTER THIRTY-NINE

Fortune and Glory

One of the guards patrolling the curtain wall of Castle Langsley sneaked a bite of cake. He was one of the unlucky guards not invited to the celebration of Princess Tara's return. With a mouthful of sweet frosting, he spotted someone in the distance.

It was Cole. He was an impressive sight indeed, mounted on a black foal, his sylvan armor glittering and the Sun Sword on his hip.

The guard dropped his slice of cake and shouted to the gatekeeper, "Open the portcullis! It's him! He's here!"

"Who?!" the gatekeeper shouted.

"Cole, the Hero of Langsley."

The celebration was fervent within the castle walls. All the people of the kingdom were invited. Peasants indulged in free casks of libations. They ate bread and cheeses and fruits they'd never tasted before. All were merry. Especially the king.

King Langsley glowed with a pride beside his impressive granddaughter, Tara I'Tir. Dressed in a beautiful white gown, she was the splitting image of his daughter. Even if she was a little distant, he knew with enough time she would come to love him.

Tara was less than thrilled to be the center of attention, and wearing a dress no less. She stared at Princes Oriel's polished crown in the hands of her nutty old grandfather. To the people of Redlund, the crown meant power. To Tara, it was a shackle.

Cole arrived at the back of the packed courtyard. He dismounted and excited children swarmed him and the unicorn.

"Careful. Diesel doesn't do well with excitement."

Diesel was the name Cole gave him. The unicorn was strong of body and stronger of will. Despite all the trouble he gave Cole on his journey back to Langsley, he was tame around the children. He allowed them to pet him and scratch his itchy body. Diesel relished love and attention and found no end of it from the children. Their parents could not understand the infatuation with the foal. All they saw was a black coated pony with odd a purple mane. But the children and a few innocent men and women in the crowd saw Diesel's glittering horn.

Cole smiled and walked through the crowd as the king began his speech. Trumpets blared and the king raised his hand. "People of Redlund! It is with great honor I am able to present to you my granddaughter, your new princess, Tara."

Ceremoniously, he raised the crown and placed it on her head. The crowd applauded. Tara Schmara. As long as they got something free to eat, they didn't care who the new princess was.

Cole stood on his toes. He saw Pal, Domina, and Macario—Maisie perched on his shoulder. They stood on stage with King Langsley and the gorgeous half-dragon princess, Tara.

"Forty long years have passed and you finally have an heir to the throne," the king bellowed. "In light of this glorious reunion, we feast and celebrate!"

The crowd erupted in applause. The king hushed the crowd. He put his hand to his heart and said, "I must thank these glorious heroes for bringing her home to me."

Domina saw Cole first. She elbowed Pal and pointed him out.

"Cole!" Pal exclaimed.

Cole made his way through the crowd, bumping into people, stepping on their toes, elbowing to get to the front of the stage. Tara kept her eyes on him like a raptor. She couldn't believe this lummox was able to defeat her father. Her father... his mission, now her mission, would have to be put on hold. Until she had revenge.

The heroes rushed to Cole and helped him up onto the stage.

Macario embraced him and said, "It brings me great pleasure that you are not dead."

"Are you sure about that?" Maisie asked.

"What about Hikari?" Domina asked.

Cole unsheathed the Sun Sword. His grim expression and silence said it all.

"I'm sorry, Cole," Pal said.

"Hikari did not die in vain," Domina said.

"Hikari died an honorable death," Cole said. "He sacrificed himself to save us. We all owe our lives to him."

"And what of the dragon?" King Langsley asked.

"Vanquished," Cole said.

Tara had enough boasting about her father's defeat and raised her dress, storming off into the castle. Before the cheerful mood was completely killed, the king spoke. "The important thing is you are still alive, and Princess Tara has returned." He turned to the crowd and announced, "Let the celebration begin!"

A band of minstrels struck up a song. Dancing and singing occupied Castle Langsley's courtyard. It was the first time in half a century.

The king threw his arm around Cole. The old man's tired eyes seemed alive with new vigor. The snow white hair, once wilted, was now groomed and puffed out like a lion's mane.

"You did well, Cole," the king said, and the dragon slayer responded with a solemn nod. "I don't know how I can ever repay you."

Pal, who had been eavesdropping, suggested, "How about you start by paying us our reward. Two hundred pounds of silver."

King Langsley pursed his lips, "Minus your advance."

Pal curtsied. "Fair enough."

King Langsley exclaimed, "Guards! Bring the heroes their reward!"

Two guards brought a large, heavy chest onto the stage. Pal opened the chest and moaned. He dipped his hand in and swirled it around the coins like a cat playing in a fishbowl.

The king clapped Cole on the back. "Congratulations. You are as wealthy as a duke."

As Cole stared at the metal coins, a heartbreaking realization dawned on him. Fortune does not bring happiness. Merely convenience. Friends and accomplishments are the real treasures in life. No amount of money could ever bring back Hikari. Cole drew in a deep and heavy breath and walked off into the castle without a word.

Pal bit one of the coins, smiled at the indentations his teeth left and tossed it back into the chest. "Looks good to me," he said with a smirk.

"That reminds me," Macario said. He took off his backpack library and removed twenty tiny sacks from one of the lower shelves. He muttered arcane words and raised his staff. The shrunken bags returned to their normal laundry-bag size.

"Are those what I think they are?" Pal asked with a smile curling up the corner of his mouth.

"The Locksmiths packed these sacks with the dragon's treasure. I shrunk them when Tara captured us. I hid them in my backpack library," Macario explained.

Pal's smile stretched from ear to ear. He hugged Macario, and said, "You're a genius! I could kiss you!"

"That will not be necessary. Pardon me, I must now make a speech." Macario cupped his lips. Using magic, he enhanced his voice like a megaphone. "People of Redlund!"

The music stopped and the entire courtyard turned their attention to the wizard on stage.

"Your ancestors mined the earth of treasures long ago, but these were taken from you by the Emerald Enormity. Now that the dragon has been slain, we give you back what is rightfully yours to inherit.

"Return this treasure in full sum,
Make things right for everyone."

Macario passed the Sylvanus Staff over the sacks. A tidal wave of priceless jewels, gemstones, and other treasures soared into the air and into the hands of the impoverished peasants of Redlund.

Pal's eyes turned to slits. "You just gave away a dragon's horde!"

"We have two hundred pounds of silver right here," Macario said.

"A dragon's horde!"

CHAPTER FORTY

To Heaven's Peak

Overcoming a swarm of butterflies in his stomach, Cole entered Tara's bedroom. There was a wardrobe, a dressing mirror, plush armchairs, and paintings that spanned the wall. In the center of the room was a princess-size bed (which, for those who don't know, is twice as big as a king's). None of it struck Cole as fitting Tara's personality at all. Not that Cole knew Tara, but from what little he did know, she didn't strike him as opulent.

Cole's eyes scanned the room for the half-dragon princess. He found her defused behind billowing white window drapes. Bent over, she leaned on the balcony in her white dress. Cole lost track of what he was doing there for a second. He stood and stared at her pleasing figure through the drapes.

Tara gazed out over her new kingdom. An orange glow washed over her from the sun setting behind the mountains of Heaven's Peak in the distance. Cole took several dry gulps, wiped his sweaty palms on his pants, and joined her on the balcony. Nervous, he stood behind her. He observed her tall, muscular body beneath the flowing white gown. Although she did not acknowledge him, she knew Cole was there. She could hear his nervous breathing.

"What do you want?" she asked in a tired and defeated tone.

"I wanted to see how you were," Cole said.

Tara smiled, but her eyes cut him like daggers. "I've been taken from my home, forced to live with a grandfather I don't know, and I'm wearing a stupid dress. I'm great."

"You look good in a dress."

"You killed my father."

"He was evil."

"Yes. But he was still my father."

This undeniable truth silenced Cole. A twinge of guilt knifed his stomach. Not for slaying Il i'Tir, but for hurting Tara's feelings without meaning to.

"Leave me," she said in an icy voice.

He wanted to express his empathy, but knew he'd never find the right words. Cole hung his head and left Tara on the balcony.

In the courtyard below, Cole pushed his way through the crowded party and overheard peasants exclaim, "Look! It's Cole! Cole the Dragon Slayer. Cole the hero! Three cheers for Cole!"

The compliments and praise he always assumed would cure his woes made little to no impression on him. He trudged through the throngs of fans, nodded thanks, and offered half-smiles in gratitude.

Macario, Maisie, Pal, and Domina sat at a long wooden banquet table in the center of the courtyard.

"Where'd you go?" Maisie asked, standing on her plate, gnawing on a chicken leg.

"To speak with Tara," Cole said.

"How did that go?" Macario asked.

"Not good," Cole said.

Pal poured him a large glass of grog, which Cole drained. Pal elbowed him, refilled his glass, and said, "Like I said, Cole, there are millions of girls in the world." Domina glared at him. "But when you find that one special girl, the rest all seem to disappear."

"Great. I found her and she hates me," Cole said. "Well, at least the people of Redlund are happy."

Cole took in the celebration and joy on the people's faces. What did it matter how he felt? They appreciated him and his friends. He was now a bonafide hero, but he had unfinished business.

Cole unsheathed the Sun Sword and held it high, admiring it. Reflections of blinding sunlight sparkled on the blade like diamonds. "My journey has just begun," he said. "I must find Hikari's brother and give him the Sun Sword."

Cole sheathed the holy katana. He bowed to his companions and retrieved Diesel. Cole and the unicorn walked to the castle portcullis. There they stopped and turned back to his friends.

Silhouetted by the sun, the burgeoning hero yelled, "So are you coming or not?"

THE END

Acknowledgements

First I must acknowledge my editor Daryl Edelman for his masterful guidance and insight. This book was a boulder in need of a sculptor. Dense and impenetrable, Daryl chiseled away the flaws and gratuities until the story hiding within revealed itself. He taught me how to polish my art and I am ever grateful.

Next, Casey Laridaen for her swift and thorough proofread. Thais Chu designed the cover and it could not be more striking. AJ Meyers developed the fantastic website. The illustrations by Rob Yulfo and Paul Kisling take my breath away every time I see them.

I thank all my friends and colleagues who read the manuscript as it evolved from a screenplay to a novel, especially Max Futterman. Rory Schwartz, thank you for your ongoing mentorship and humor. Richard and Mica Hadar, you are the embodiment of generosity. Max Kaufman and Aaron Hornick, your friendship and loyalty are beyond measure.

To my other family, John and Beth, thank you for opening your home to me and nourishing my creativity and health. Meaghan, Patrick, and Luke, I thank you for welcoming me despite my desire to steal the spotlight.

Matthew, this story is the culmination of so many brothers' nights where you let me spit ideas at you and then gave me feedback. Anna, your unending love, and belief in me makes me proud to be your big brother. Grandma Gloria and Susan, I wish you were here to enjoy this tale. I miss you both every day.

Mom and Dad, I am so proud to share this story with the world. You always gave me the opportunity to pursue my dreams, no matter the sacrifice. You are the heroes in my life.

Finally, Briana, my loving wife. You pushed me to get this book out of my laptop and into the world. Without you, this book would still be a document in Word. You give me courage, motivate, and inspire me daily. My life would be incomplete without you. I don't say it often enough so here it is in writing, forever.

ABOUT THE AUTHOR

Born and raised in Brooklyn, New York, A.D. Greer lives in Sunnyside, Queens with his wife and their adorable cocker spaniel. The Legends of Eld: The Dragon of Elfwood is his first novel.

For more information on your favorite characters, new books in the series, and upcoming events, visit www.LegendsOfEld.com